W9-BFJ-087

3pts.

WITHDRAWN

Library Media Center
Fegely Middle School

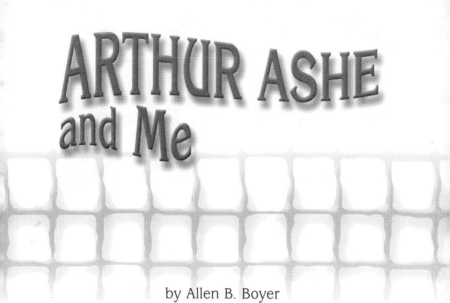

ARTHUR ASHE
and Me

by Allen B. Boyer

SUMMIT BOOKS

Perfection Learning®

Cover Illustration: Dan Hatala
Inside Illustration: Dan Hatala

About the Author

Allen Boyer lives just outside of Hershey,
Pennsylvania, with his wife, Suzanne. Having a father
who loved the game of tennis, Mr. Boyer began playing
at an early age and continues to play today.

Mr. Boyer first became interested in writing while
taking a class in college. He received his undergraduate
degree from Millersville University and his master's
degree in education from Penn State. *Arthur Ashe and
Me* is his first novel.

Dedication

For Terry Wallace, who planted the seed to write.
For my parents, who nurtured its growth.
And to my wife, for all her love and for always believing.

Text © 2003 by **Perfection Learning® Corporation**.
All rights reserved. No part of this book may be reproduced,
stored in a retrieval system, or transmitted in any form or by
any means, electronic, mechanical, photocopying, recording,
or otherwise, without prior permission of the publisher.
Printed in the United States of America.

For information, contact
Perfection Learning® Corporation
1000 North Second Avenue, P.O. Box 500
Logan, Iowa 51546-0500.
Phone: 1-800-831-4190
Fax: 1-800-543-2745
perfectionlearning.com

Paperback ISBN 0-7891-5855-8
Cover Craft® ISBN 0-7569-0973-2

Dear Meredith,

I'm sorry for what happened to you.

I'm sorry for causing you so much pain.

I'm sorry I can't choose the right words
to tell you how bad I feel. The only
words I can think of are the ones I've
used over and over. I'm sorry. I'm
sorry. I'm sorry.

Faith

1

Faith Long didn't talk much. She had grown very quiet exactly six months ago. Her teachers were concerned. They wrote letters to her parents, who agreed to have her meet with a guidance counselor a couple of times. She even ate lunch with the principal once. All of them asked the same questions. How was she doing? Did she get along with her parents? Did she know what it meant to be depressed?

Chapter One

Now that school was over and summer vacation was starting, Faith could escape the questions. Being on vacation also meant she could stay up late at night and watch TV. And she could close her curtains to keep the daylight out in the morning. The darkness helped her sleep a little longer and avoid the day.

This morning, the daylight softly slipped between her curtains and struck the tennis trophies that lined the shelf above her desk. The awards caught the morning light and cast a dull gold reflection that filled Faith's room.

She stirred, then her brown eyes opened and squinted at the light. She closed her eyes again and tried to return to the darkness. She tried to erase the image of the glowing trophies from her mind. After a few moments, she could see the trophies in her sleep. Finally, she hopped out of bed, flung open the curtains, and surrendered to the day.

Faith yawned and stared out the window for a moment. The sky was as blue as a robin's egg. The yard was green and neatly trimmed. She could smell fresh grass clippings in the air and guessed that her dad had just mowed. The trees whispered in the passing breeze that rolled by her window.

She wondered what time it was and turned to look at her clock. Her eyes stopped at the collection of tennis trophies shimmering in the light. Faith walked over to her desk and picked up the biggest one. She held it in her hands and turned it in the light. She could feel her heart begin to pound harder with each second she held it. Her throat became dry. Tears filled her eyes. She turned to the closet, opened it, and placed the trophy in a box on the floor. Stopping to wipe away the tears, she returned to the desk.

One by one, she picked up each trophy and placed it in the box in her closet. When the last trophy was gone, she closed the box and shoved it as far back in the darkness as she could. Then she closed the closet door and crawled back into bed. Lying there, Faith just stared at the empty shelves above her desk.

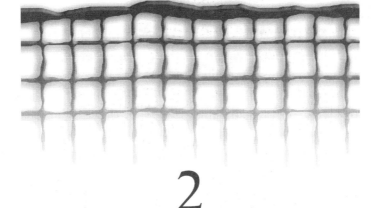

2

"Morning, sleepyhead," Hank Long greeted his daughter. Sitting at the kitchen table, he peeked over the morning paper and smiled at Faith.

Mr. Long was a gym teacher at the local high school. He loved to play sports and had gotten Faith interested in tennis when she was six. He always got up with the sun—even during summer vacation.

Faith's mother, on the other hand, was a night owl. She liked to stay up late and then sleep in.

Faith had always wondered if that was one of the reasons her parents had gotten a divorce. When she'd asked her mom, she'd learned it was the "little things" that led to the divorce. Faith still wondered what that meant.

"Hey, Dad," Faith said. She grabbed a glass from the cupboard and poured herself some juice.

"So," Mr. Long began, putting his paper down, "you're on vacation. Gonna sleep your summer away?"

"No, Dad," Faith sighed, taking a sip of juice.

"Just wondering if you had any plans, honey," he said. "Anything you really wanted to do this summer?"

"Not really." Faith shrugged. "Just wanna do my own thing."

"Faith," Mr. Long said, pushing his paper to the side, "your mom's been calling me ever since you told her you wanted to spend the summer here. She wants me to make sure this summer is a special one. You sure you don't have any ideas?"

"No," Faith mumbled. "Like I said, Dad, just do my own thing."

"And what exactly is that?"

"Anything but tennis," Faith sighed, rolling her eyes. "Anything but traveling around the country playing tennis tournaments. This summer, I want to watch TV. Read some books. Surf the Net. Just have a normal summer like other kids do."

"Look, honey," Mr. Long began, "I'm gonna work around the house a lot this summer. I'm not planning any big trips for us. Can't afford it anyway. If you want a summer to figure out some things, that's fine with me. I know you had a hard year at school. I'll give you all the room you need to think about everything."

"Thanks, Dad," Faith mumbled.

"I just have one suggestion," Mr. Long advised.

Chapter Two

"What's that?" Faith asked, holding her breath.

"There's a tennis club just a block from here," Mr. Long said. "It's just two clay courts by an old barn. It's called the Green Leaf Tennis Club. Mostly a bunch of old doctors and lawyers play there. I know the owner, Jack West. He's a nice guy. I told him all about you."

"Geez, Dad," Faith said, a little embarrassed.

"Hey," Mr. Long said, putting his paper down, "your mom and I understand you've had a tough time. But the bottom line is we agreed that we don't want you to spend your summer sitting around feeling sorry for yourself. We both want you to do something. Anything."

"You and mom agreed—that doesn't happen much," Faith muttered to herself. She took a sip from her glass and put it down on the counter. "Whatever you're thinking, I hope it doesn't involve tennis. I *don't* want to play at that tennis club—or anywhere else for that matter."

"I wasn't talking to Mr. West about you *playing* tennis," Mr. Long explained. "I was talking to him about you *working* for him this summer."

"Working?" Faith asked. She rinsed out her glass in the sink. "You want me to get a job? I don't wanna spend my summer working, Dad."

"It would be an easy way to make some money," Mr. Long replied. "All you have to do is take care of the courts. You'd water them and brush them every day. Mr. West will pay you ten dollars a day. Not bad for about an hour's work."

"TEN DOLLARS!" Faith exclaimed. She did the math in her head and laughed when the total popped up. "SEVENTY DOLLARS A WEEK! This is so cool! Do I get to keep all the money? When does he want me to start? Do I work in the morning or the evening?" Faith rambled.

Then another thought popped into her head. "I'm gonna have the coolest clothes!" she said.

"So you're interested?" Mr. Long grinned, amazed at the instant change in his daughter.

"Totally!" Faith laughed.

"If you'd like," Mr. Long suggested, "we can walk down to the club. I can introduce you to Mr. West. He likes to talk, so we might be there awhile."

"Let me put on my tennis shoes," Faith said. She walked over to her dad and hugged him. "You're the best, Dad. Ya know that?"

"It's nice to hear sometimes," Mr. Long said. "Better get those shoes. I'll meet you outside."

3

Faith and her dad walked for about a block. The paved street curved under a series of tall trees. The branches stretched over the road, forming a cover of green. As they walked beneath the trees, Faith noticed that the paved road turned into a path of loose stones and dirt. They followed the stone road to a small wooden bridge built over a creek.

Faith watched her dad cross the bridge and walk up a hill to a barn. She stopped to look at the creek. The water was clear and rolled slowly over the rocks and stones in the creek bed. She closed her eyes and listened to the soft sound the water made when it flowed under her. It was such a quiet place, she thought. It seemed like the kind of place that would listen to her secrets and keep them forever.

"Hey, Faith!" she heard her dad shout. She opened her eyes and noticed her dad standing in front of a large barn. Next to him stood an old man with bright white hair. He was wearing baggy blue pants with suspenders and a white shirt.

Faith looked down at the creek once more and then turned and sprinted up the hill.

"Mr. West, this is my daughter, Faith," Mr. Long proudly announced when she reached them.

"Pleasure to meet you," Mr. West said, chomping on a pipe. He held out his hand and smiled. His blue eyes sparkled through the thin layer of smoke. "Welcome to the Green Leaf Tennis Club—the only tennis club in Pennsylvania with international clay courts."

"What do you mean by '*international* clay courts'?" Faith asked. She'd played tennis on clay courts before. She knew that it was like playing on dirt. Her shoes and socks got dirty. The balls got dirty. When the wind blew, she'd gotten clay in her eyes. All in all, she didn't like playing on clay courts that much. So what made these so special?

"We purchase the clay from a tennis club in France," Mr. West explained. "Then we mix the clay with brick dust and spread it on the court. You won't find two more beautiful tennis courts in the state."

"That's amazing." Mr. Long grinned. "All the way from France. Isn't that amazing, Faith?"

"Yes, Dad," Faith moaned. Her dad seemed excited enough for both of them, Faith thought. She turned to Mr. West and tried to smile. "So what would I do here?"

"Come with me and I'll show you," Mr. West said. He turned with small steps and slowly began walking up the hill. Faith followed her dad and Mr. West, trying to ignore the pipe smoke blowing in her face.

"Why did they build the tennis courts here, Jack?" Mr. Long asked. "You have to admit it's a bit odd building tennis courts by a barn."

"This land has been in my family for 200 years," Mr. West explained. He paused and then puffed on his pipe for a few seconds. "When I fought in World War II, I met a guy who played tennis. He made it sound fun. So after the war, some of my friends and I decided to build these courts. My dad gave me permission to build them on the family land. So we bought some bricks, dug up the land, and built them in about a week."

Faith walked quietly behind her dad and Mr. West. She thought Mr. West seemed pretty nice. He had a soft voice and tended to scratch his head while he talked. She thought it was funny hearing an old man like Mr. West talk about getting permission from his dad to do something. Faith's parents usually let her do what she wanted, even if it meant not playing tennis.

At the top of the hill, Faith could see the two clay tennis courts. Without warning, her legs froze and she stopped walking. She just stared at the courts for a few seconds. They were the first courts she'd seen in six months. Suddenly, it seemed strange to be this close again.

"Faith," her dad said, "c'mon, honey."

"I'm coming," Faith answered. The world seemed to slow down for a moment. She looked at her feet. Then she took a deep breath and walked onto one of the courts. Her eyes lingered on every detail—the bright white lines, the net strung across the middle, the fence surrounding the court. Faith took it all in and felt her stomach grow sick.

"Let me show you something," Mr. West said, smiling. He shuffled over to the fence and pointed to a pair of brooms leaning there. He turned to Faith and took the pipe out of his mouth.

"You use the wide broom to sweep both courts. Sweep away any marks or footprints. When you're finished, use this little broom to sweep the dirt off the lines."

"Is that all?" Faith asked. "I mean—is that all you want me to do?"

"Pretty much," Mr. West replied. He put his pipe back in his mouth and smiled. "If it doesn't rain for a couple of days, you may need to water the courts with a hose. But I'll help you with that. It's kind of tricky since we pump the water up from the creek.

"Now I'll need you here every day at sunset to sweep," he finished. "Will that work for you?"

"Sure." Faith nodded.

"Then you can start tomorrow," Mr. West said. He turned and headed for the dirt path. Faith and Mr. Long followed him. When they reached the barn, Mr. West walked inside. Faith and her dad waited outside, not sure what he was doing.

"Here," Mr. West said, walking out of the barn. He handed Faith a small coffee can.

"What is it?" Faith asked, a little confused. "Do you want me to make coffee too?"

"No," Mr. West laughed. He took off his glasses, rubbed his blue eyes, and then put his glasses back on. "Little too hot for that. Go ahead and open it. See what's inside."

Faith pulled off the lid. When she looked inside, she was surprised to see the can was filled with dry corn. She dipped her hand inside and scooped some of it out. The corn felt hard and cool in her hand. She dropped it back into the can and looked at Mr. West, unsure what to do with it.

"Is this for the courts?" she guessed. She looked at her dad, who just shook his head. He seemed as confused as she was.

"No," Mr. West replied. He pointed to a large oak tree a few feet from the barn. "Take a handful and throw it over there."

Faith dipped her hand into the can and scooped out as much corn as she could get. Some of it slipped between her fingers and dropped back into the can. Turning, she walked over to the tree. She tossed the corn into the shade as if throwing a coin into a water fountain. Everything but the wish, she thought.

Suddenly two squirrels charged down from the tree and dove into the grass. They raced around, quickly consuming the corn. Then a third squirrel jumped down from another tree and dove into the pile of corn. Faith smiled as she watched the squirrels run and bump into one another while they ate the corn. When the last piece of corn was gone, the squirrels began to chase one another. Two of them collided and then scrambled into the field. The third climbed back up the tree.

"They're so cute," Faith said.

"This is a special place," Mr. West said. "If you look hard enough, you'll find some magic around here."

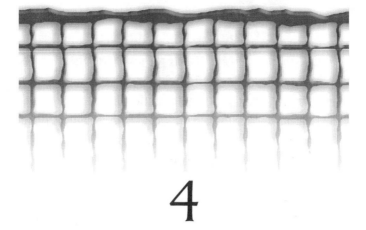

4

The next day, Faith walked down to the tennis club after supper. She was anxious to start her job, even though she knew the sun wouldn't be setting for a long time. She walked down the stone road, under the tunnel of trees, and stopped on the wooden bridge.

Leaning over the railing, she looked down at the water. Faith reached for her necklace. She grabbed hold of the half-heart charm that dangled from a chain. The longer she held it, the more she began to think about last summer. The necklace and the charm had been a gift from a friend. Someone she hadn't seen in a long time. Still, whenever she wore the necklace, she thought of their friendship and how it was lost. Faith took full responsibility for what had happened. She knew it was her fault they weren't friends anymore. The necklace reminded her of that fact too.

The water below was calm. The trees were still. Silence surrounded her. Faith remembered her secrets. Her mind drifted back to something that had happened the last time she'd stood on a tennis court. The memory was still sharp in her mind. She found that when she thought about it too long, this particular memory could still bite her and bring back the pain.

"I'm sorry," she whispered, rubbing the necklace between her fingers. She felt her eyes fill with tears. Lowering her head, she watched one tear drop gently into the cleansing creek waters below. Wherever the creek carried her tear, she thought, it wouldn't change what had happened last winter. It wouldn't change the pain she'd accidentally caused someone else. Faith sighed and watched the water curl around the rocks.

Suddenly, through the sweet sounds of rippling water, she began to hear voices. Talking and laughter floated in the distance. Faith looked up at the barn and walked off the bridge. She heard the laughter again. As she reached the top of the hill, she noticed two sports cars parked in front of the barn. When she got to the barn, she saw two men playing on the court.

"That was a lucky shot!" one man called out.

"It's skill, Dan. I'm sure that's what you meant to say!" the other man replied.

Both men laughed out loud. One of the men had long dark hair that was pulled back into a ponytail. He wore glasses and had braces on both of his knees. The second man was older, with white hair and a round belly that made it look as if he had a beach ball stuffed under his white tennis shirt.

The white-haired man ran for a shot. As he reached for the ball, he looked as if he were going to lose his balance and fall. Faith held her breath while she watched him swing wildly and smack the ball over the fence and into the field. The long-haired man began to laugh. Then he spotted Faith. The smile left his face as he walked across the court to her.

"This is private property," he stated loudly, pointing his racket at Faith.

"Yes," Faith said. "I—"

"You're trespassing," the long-haired man interrupted. He looked over his glasses at her. "Clearly you shouldn't be here."

"I—I—" Faith tried to say. She stopped, took a deep breath, and tried to relax. "I work here."

"You?" the man laughed. "Don't lie to me, young lady," he accused.

"I'm not," Faith replied. She tried to stay calm, but she could feel her heart pounding and her hands shaking a little.

"I'm the president of the club. If anyone hired you, it would have been me."

"Mr. West hired me to sweep the courts," Faith explained.

"I see," the man said slowly and nodded. He looked at Faith but didn't smile. "Jack finally decided to take my advice. Only I told him to hire one of the guys from the high school football team. How long ago did he talk to you?"

"Yesterday."

"What's your name?" the man asked.

"Faith."

"I'm Doctor Sipe," the long-haired man replied. He pointed across the court at his opponent. "That's Doctor Pruitt."

"Hi," Faith said with a smile. She waved at the old man on the court. The man merely nodded at her, keeping his hands on his hips and continuing to breathe hard.

"Now," Doctor Sipe began, "Doctor Pruitt just hit one of my tennis balls over the fence and into the cornfield. It'll be easy to find because it has my name on it."

"Your name on it?" Faith blurted out.

"Yes." Doctor Sipe grinned. "I put my name on all my tennis balls. Makes it easier to find them if they get lost. Now be a dear and go get that ball for us."

"But I just came to sweep the courts," Faith protested.

"As you can see," Doctor Sipe sighed, "we're still playing our match. You can't sweep the courts until

20

we're done. Unless your time is more important than ours—in which case we'll just leave right now," he said sarcastically. "Now, may we finish our match?"

"Of course," Faith mumbled.

"Thanks," Doctor Sipe snapped, quickly returning to his position on the court. He pointed toward the field and shouted, "Don't forget to look for my ball."

The cornstalks were high. Faith found a path between two stalks. The corn towered over her. She looked up but could only see the violet and crimson clouds that swirled in the sky above her. She turned her eyes toward the ground and tried to find the ball in what little light was left in the day. She pushed aside one of the stalks, stepped around another, and then spotted the yellow tennis ball on the ground. She could see the name SIPE clearly printed in bright red letters on the ball.

"Got you!" Faith declared and quickly walked over to where it was. Without warning, a dark shadow seemed to move over the ball for a brief moment. When the shadow passed, the ball was gone.

Faith stopped in her tracks and stared at the dirt in disbelief. She reached down and felt the ground for any clues to the missing ball.

"Have you found it yet?" Doctor Sipe called out.

"I . . ." Faith began, pulling a fistful of dirt out of the ground and letting it run through her fingers. The ball had vanished right in front of her eyes. Slowly,

Faith backed out of the field. Her eyes continued to scan the ground, looking for any signs of the tennis ball. Suddenly, she felt herself back into something warm and wet and breathing. She spun around to face Doctor Sipe.

"Did you find my ball?" he repeated, looking down at her through his glasses.

"I thought I did," Faith mumbled, stepping away from him. "I guess I was wrong."

"Most disappointing," Doctor Sipe sighed. He wiped the sweat from his forehead and stared down at Faith.

"I—I'm sorry, Doctor Sipe," Faith said.

"I'll be watching you," he warned. He waved his finger at Faith and then stepped back onto the tennis court. He turned to Doctor Pruitt. "Send a girl to do a boy's job and lose a tennis ball. I may have to talk to Jack about her. I think he owes me a new tennis ball. How about it?"

"Worth a shot," Doctor Pruitt laughed. "Don't be too hard on the old man though. If he drops over from a heart attack, we'll lose this land and the club. Don't go raining on everyone's parade for some stupid tennis ball."

"It's not the tennis ball," Doctor Sipe argued. "It's the principle of it!"

"Fine," Doctor Pruitt sighed. "Let's get back to the game."

Faith turned back toward the field. She wanted to

cry, but she wouldn't. She remembered the last two times she'd cried. The first was last year when she'd found out her parents were getting a divorce. She'd cried so hard that day, she didn't think she'd have any tears left. Yet, what happened six months ago had made her feel even worse, and she'd found new tears to cry.

Now she took a few steps into the field and looked one last time for the ball. It was nowhere to be found. When she came out of the field, Doctor Sipe and Doctor Pruitt had left the court. She took down the long broom from the fence and began to sweep both courts. She pushed the broom in front of her, moving from one side to the other until every inch of the court had been swept. When she finished, she grabbed the smaller broom and swept the lines on the court.

As she hung the smaller broom on the fence, she turned to the field one last time. A breeze passed over the cornstalks, causing them to sway. Faith listened closely. All she could hear was a cricket chirping faintly.

Part of her wanted to believe she'd been seeing things when the black shadow took the tennis ball. But part of her knew it had been real. Faith knew there was something hiding out there. Something that had Doctor Sipe's tennis ball.

5

The next morning, Faith returned to the tennis club. Walking up the stone road, she spotted Mr. West sitting on a chair in front of the barn. His head was down, as if he were looking at something on his lap. When she got closer, Faith could see he was holding a book. She also noticed his eyes were closed.

"Mr. West," Faith said softly. His eyes stayed closed. She stepped closer and tapped him on the shoulder.

"Mr. West," she said a little louder.

"Huh?" Mr. West jumped. He looked around, a little confused. "Oh . . . Faith . . . I must have fallen asleep. What time is it?"

"Ten o'clock," Faith replied.

"Oh, my," Mr. West sighed. He rubbed his eyes and smiled at Faith. "You're here a little early today."

"Thought maybe I could do some extra work," Faith said. She looked around. "Is there anything you need help with?"

"I might have something for you," Mr. West said. He took off his glasses and held them up to the light. "If you don't mind me asking—wouldn't you rather be with your friends? A day like this should be spent at the pool, don't you think?"

"I don't have any friends around here," Faith explained. "I live in Florida."

"Oh, yes," Mr. West said. "Your dad did say you were here just for the summer."

"Yes, sir," Faith said. "I came up here to spend the summer with my dad. He's a teacher, so he doesn't work during the summer. Since Mom works, I thought it would be fun to spend the summer here."

"Your father is very proud of you," Mr. West said. He says you're one heck of a tennis player. Said you were ranked number one in the country for your age group. Is that true?"

"Yeah," Faith muttered, looking down at the ground. "I don't play anymore, though."

"Really? Why?" He looked surprised.

"I'd rather not say," Faith said.

"I see," Mr. West said. He took out his handkerchief and cleaned his glasses. "I talked to Doctor Sipe this morning. He said you lost one of his tennis balls."

"That's not what happened," Faith protested.

"Why would Doctor Sipe lie?"

"I don't know," Faith said. "But you have to believe me, Mr. West. I didn't take his tennis ball. Doctor Pruitt hit it into the field, and Doctor Sipe sent me to look for it. When I couldn't find it, he got mad. That's what happened."

"I see," Mr. West said and nodded. He took out his pipe, lit it, and began to make small clouds of smoke with each puff.

"Don't you believe me?"

"I believe two things," Mr. West began. "I know I should only believe half of everything that Doctor Sipe tells me."

"And the second thing?" Faith asked.

"That a promise is a promise," Mr. West said. He struggled to get out of the chair. Faith grabbed his arm and helped him up. When he got his balance, he led Faith up the small path to the tennis courts. Faith held her breath while she walked behind him and the smoke.

When they reached the courts, Mr. West turned to

Faith. "Did you sweep these courts yesterday?"

"Yes," Faith replied. She looked over and saw that the courts were marked up. It wasn't the way she had left them. Someone had been playing on the them. She pointed to the courts and turned to Mr. West.

"I swept them," she said. "This isn't what they looked like when I left. There weren't any marks on them at all. Honest."

"Like I said, Faith, I believe a promise is a promise," Mr. West stated. "I love these courts more than anything, but I'm too old to care for them. I'm counting on you to do it. Please make sure they're swept at the end of every day—or I'm going to have to find someone else to work here. Do you understand?"

"Yes, sir," Faith said. She looked down at the clay courts and the marks that spotted them. She turned to the big broom hanging on the fence, took it down, and began to drag it across the courts again. She looked back at Mr. West, who was quietly walking back down the hill to the barn. She watched until all that was left was the smoke lingering behind him.

Faith felt bad for letting Mr. West down. But she didn't know what had happened. Maybe Doctor Sipe had come back after she left and played some more. He didn't seem very nice. Maybe he wanted to make trouble for her. Or maybe someone else had come later and played. Either way, she knew she would be back this evening to check on the courts and sweep them again if necessary.

Faith dragged the broom back to the fence. Then she turned and walked across the court to the field. She stooped down and looked into the field. She was kind of scared to go in after yesterday, but she felt as if she needed to find Doctor Sipe's tennis ball. She tried to remember exactly where she'd walked to look for the ball.

The wind blew, and the corn waved. The world seemed to grow silent. Then she heard a voice as soft as the wind. "Thank you."

"Who said that?" Faith asked. She looked around, frantically searching for the source of the voice. She shook her head and figured she had imagined it. When she looked back into the field, she saw something round tucked in the shadows. Taking a few steps into the field, she bent down to see what it was. It was Doctor Sipe's tennis ball!

"Oh my gosh," she whispered. She reached down and picked up the ball. It felt firm and new. It was stained with clay from the tennis courts. Faith brushed off the ball and stood up. Her thoughts drifted back to the voice she'd thought she'd heard. She looked around but couldn't see anyone. As far as Faith could tell, she was all alone.

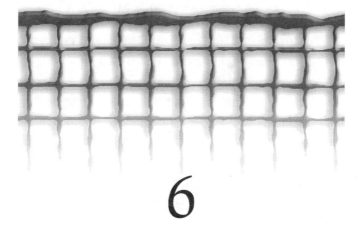

6

Mr. Long spent most of the morning painting the front door. It was one of the many summer projects he told Faith he wanted to finish over the next three months. He took a step back and smiled at the fresh coat of white paint.

"Looks good, Dad."

Mr. Long turned to see Faith standing behind him. She was tossing Doctor Sipe's tennis ball in one hand. She smiled slightly. The sunlight caught Faith's long brown hair, casting a glow around her. She looked happier than she had in a long time, Mr. Long noticed.

"Where were you?" he asked.

"At the club," Faith replied.

"Thought you only had to work after supper?"

"I do," Faith said. "Just went up to check on things."

"So do you like it?" Mr. Long asked, cleaning off one of his brushes with a rag.

"Yeah," Faith answered. "Mr. West is pretty cool."

"That's good," Mr. Long said. He looked down at the brush he was wiping off.

"You okay, Dad?"

"Well . . . I went in your room this morning," Mr. Long began slowly. He kept his eyes on the brush he was holding. "I did a load of wash and was putting your clothes away. I noticed that your tennis trophies were gone. Do know what happened to them?"

The smile faded from Faith's face. She dropped the ball on the ground and watched it bounce under a bush next to the porch. She stared at the porch, folded her arms, and sighed.

"I put them away, Dad."

"Where?" Mr. Long asked.

"I put them in a box in the closet," Faith said, her voice starting to quiver. She could feel her eyes begin to well up with tears. She rubbed her eyes and watched her dad put his paintbrush down on the porch. He crossed the porch and put his arms around her.

"I'm sorry, Faith," he apologized and squeezed her tightly. "They were the only things of yours that I had after the divorce. I just wanted you to feel at home. If you want to keep them in the closet, that's fine with me."

"Thanks, Dad," Faith said. They were silent for a moment.

"Your mom called while you were gone," Mr.

Long said, breaking the silence. "She asked how you were doing. She wants you to call her. She misses you."

"I'll call her tonight," Faith promised.

"Good," Mr. Long said. He turned back to his painting.

Faith looked down for the ball. Her eyes scanned the bright green grass. She walked over to the bush and kneeled down to look for the tennis ball. She saw bugs, dried leaves, and weeds—but no tennis ball.

"Dad," Faith began, "did you see where the ball went?"

"Yeah," Mr. Long replied. He put down his brush and walked over to the bush. "Saw it go under there. Why?"

"I can't find it," Faith said. She was on her hands and knees, looking under the bush. Her hand sank into something soft and wet and she quickly pulled back. "Its gotta be here!"

"Maybe a squirrel ran off with it," Mr. Long laughed.

"I know it's here!" Faith shouted, digging under the bush again.

"You don't have to get upset. It'll turn up."

"It's the second time in two days I've lost this ball," Faith complained. She stood up and brushed the dirt from her knees. "Doesn't it bother you?"

"Doesn't *what* bother me?" Mr. Long asked.

"That the tennis ball just disappeared?"

"I'm sure it's around here somewhere," Mr. Long said. He handed her some old rags. "Here. Help me clean up, and we'll have some lunch. You can look for the ball later."

"Fine," Faith said grumpily. She hopped up onto the porch and helped her dad pick up some brushes and cans. As they walked into the house, she kept her eye on the bush. She couldn't believe the ball had disappeared again!

Faith spent most of the day helping her dad around the house. Together they finished the door and began to paint the porch. The topic of tennis—or the lost ball—didn't come up again.

After supper, Faith slipped out the door and walked down the street to the stone road. When she reached the bridge, she paused to look at the sunset flickering off the water. As she watched the creek, she heard a sound. She turned and looked up the hill.

It was the sound of a tennis ball being hit. But the popping sounds weren't close enough together for it to be two people hitting to each other. The occasional "pops" indicated a tennis ball being whacked by a single player.

As she walked up the hill, Faith noticed that the sky was growing dark. The long shadows from the trees stretched across the grass. The sky was turning a dark shade of violet. It was too dark to play tennis, she thought. The courts had lights, but she could see they weren't turned on. There weren't any cars parked in front of the barn either. Who was playing tennis?

She made her way up to the barn. The popping sounds were getting louder. Every five or ten seconds, she heard another "pop" echo down from the courts. She hurried to the dirt path that wound alongside the barn and up to the courts. When she reached the end of the path, she stopped and looked around.

Both courts were empty. Three tennis balls lay on one court. Faith picked up the balls and then noticed the ball marks on the clay court. Where was the player?

"Hello!" Faith called out. Only the crickets in the field chirped in reply.

She shrugged and grabbed the big broom off the fence and began to pull it around both courts. As she swept, she began to notice something strange. While there were lots of ball marks on the court, there weren't any footprints!

"This is so weird," Faith mumbled to herself. "I know I heard someone playing."

When she finished sweeping the courts, Faith looked around one more time. She scanned the tall stalks of corn next to the courts and paused. The field is the only place where someone could run and hide, she thought.

The sun was down now. The violet sky was turning black. Darkness was beginning to surround her. She wanted to look in the field, but it seemed too creepy in the dark. Besides, she thought, if there *was* something in there taking the tennis balls, she didn't want to run into it.

Suddenly she felt something strange come over her. She felt as if she were being watched. Faith squinted hard and looked around. She stepped back from the field. She was sure a pair of eyes were looking right at her, but she couldn't find them.

"It's nothing," she told herself, trying to stay calm. She left the courts and walked down the path to the barn. A patch of golden light filled one of the barn's windows. Faith noticed that a light had been left on inside the barn. Was someone in there? Was it the person she'd heard playing?

Faith had never gone into the barn before. She didn't even know if she was allowed to. Still, the door stood wide open, inviting her inside.

"Just a quick peek," she told herself and stepped inside. A cobweb greeted her as she walked through the doorway. It tangled in her hair, and she quickly brushed it off. She prayed she wouldn't feel anything crawling in her hair.

Faith glanced around at the wood walls and floor. A couch and chairs were scattered about. A refrigerator quietly hummed in a corner. The light that had been left on was a floor lamp next to the couch. A giant green rug was spread across the center of the room.

What interested Faith the most were the pictures that hung on the wall. They were black and white photos of tennis players. Faith guessed that they had been members of the club.

She noticed that one picture was of a dark-haired Mr. West standing on a tennis court dressed in shorts and a white shirt. His smile was the same, but he was thinner and younger. It seemed kind of strange, Faith thought, to be looking at pictures of old men when they were young. She even found Doctor Sipe. In the picture, he had very short hair and no glasses. They had all changed over the years, Faith thought.

The last picture was a group shot of all the tennis players when they were younger. The only thing that hadn't changed was that they still loved the game.

As Faith left the barn, she felt something spark inside her. A brief flicker of hope burned. Maybe one day she could learn to love tennis again. Maybe she'd be able to enjoy the game for as long as the members of the Green Leaf Tennis Club.

7

A week went by and Faith began to enjoy spending more and more time at the tennis club. She got to meet some of the club's members. She especially liked two old men who always introduced themselves to her as "Norton and Norton." That was the name of their law firm. Their first names were Stan and Sam.

Norton and Norton were identical twins. Both were short with round stomachs and short legs. Both heads were bald with white hair around the sides. What Faith liked most about the brothers was that they were always laughing and joking. They had fun from the time they arrived at the club till the time they left.

One evening, while Faith was waiting to sweep, Norton and Norton were playing a tennis match against Doctor Pruitt and Doctor Sipe. One of the Nortons sprinted for a shot, tripped over his feet, and fell to the court in a cloud of dust. Faith sprinted out to the court to help.

"You okay?" Sam asked his brother as he and Faith pulled him to a stand.

"It's my ankle," Stan replied. "I think I sprained it. I can't finish."

"Lean on me," Faith said. She helped him over to a bench next to the courts. When he sat down, she noticed that the front of his shirt was covered with bright red clay—especially the part of his shirt covering his large stomach.

"Are you okay?" Doctor Pruitt asked, jogging over to the bench.

"Yeah, it just needs some ice," Stan said, wincing at the pain.

"Tough break, Norton!" Doctor Sipe called out from the court. He walked up to the net and smiled. "Guess we win!"

"Rats!" Stan grunted. "One more point and we would have won."

"Like I said," Doctor Sipe grinned, "tough break."

"I have an idea," Stan suggested. "Let Faith substitute for me."

"What?" Doctor Sipe laughed.

"What?" Faith said at the same time. She stood up straight and stepped back.

"Here," Mr. Norton said and grinned. "Take my racket. Jack West said you used to play. Just serve the ball and play for one point. It's okay. Just try it."

"I—I can't," Faith mumbled. She reached down and grabbed the half-heart charm that hung from her necklace. She rubbed it between her fingers.

"She's scared, Stan," Doctor Sipe said. "Let's go down and get something to drink, fellas. I'll get Stan some ice."

"No, wait," Stan said, handing his racket to Faith. "Here. Just one point, Faith."

"Come on, Faith," Sam pleaded. "It'll be fun. Just try it."

"I . . ." Faith tried to speak, but nothing came out.

"Splendid!" the Nortons said together, pushing the racket into her hand.

Sam pushed Faith onto the court. Doctor Sipe and Doctor Pruitt smiled at each other and then walked back onto the court. Faith walked to the back of the court, still getting used to the feeling of holding a tennis racket again. Slowly she picked up one of the tennis balls. It felt soft and fuzzy in her hand. She put her toe up to the line and looked across the net at Doctor Sipe. He was staring at her, which made her a little nervous.

"Ready when you are!" Doctor Sipe called out. Faith tossed the ball into the air and swung the racket as hard as she could. When she hit the ball, it made a loud "pop" sound. She watched Doctor Sipe swing at her shot but miss it completely.

The Nortons cheered.

"Spectacular shot!" Stan called out from the sideline.

"Wonderful hit!" Sam yelled from the net.

"I've gotta sweep the courts now," Faith said. She walked off the court and handed the racket to the injured Norton.

"My dear," Stan Norton laughed, "where did you learn to hit the ball like that?"

Faith said nothing. She just turned and walked away. She looked over her shoulder one time to see Doctor Sipe glaring at her though his glasses. She grabbed the broom from the fence and began to sweep the court.

"Make sure you sweep every spot," Doctor Sipe grumbled to Faith. He stopped and glared at her again. "I'll check them before I leave. They'd better be perfect."

Faith slowly began to push the large broom over the court. She couldn't believe what she'd just done. Why had she done it? Why had she taken the tennis racket? The Nortons had made it seem so simple, she reasoned. And, she admitted to herself, deep down inside, she'd wanted to beat Doctor Sipe. But now she realized that she'd only made him madder at her.

Nothing good ever came from winning, Faith thought.

Dear Meredith,

I've decided not to play tennis this summer. Instead, I'm staying with my dad, catching up on some reading, and working at a tennis club not far from my house. I told my dad that I don't want to play tennis anymore. I just don't care about it. It's not important. Winning isn't important. He thinks what happened to you wasn't my fault, but I know it was.

Faith

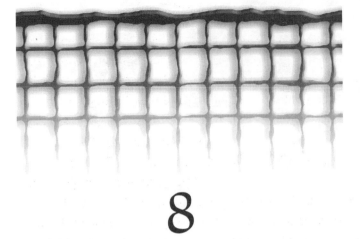

8

The next morning, Faith's dad woke her up. She yawned and looked out the window. She could tell by the cool morning air that it was early. Rubbing her eyes, Faith tried to focus on what her dad was saying.

"A Doctor Sipe is on the phone," Mr. Long explained. "He says the courts weren't swept last night. Did you forget to do them?"

"No," Faith yawned. "He's just mad because I beat him in a tennis match."

"You played tennis!" Mr. Long said.

"It was just one point," Faith mumbled, sitting up in bed. "Tell him I'll go up later."

"He wants to know if you can do it now."

"He's mean," Faith said. "He has this long ponytail, and he . . . he just gives me the creeps."

"I think you should go now," Mr. Long suggested.

He walked over to her window and pushed the curtains to the side. The room filled with light.

"Dad!" Faith squealed, pulling the covers over her head.

"It'll be good to get your day started early for a change," Mr. Long said. "You go up to the club and sweep, and I'll scramble up some eggs for us."

"But, Dad!" Faith grumbled.

"C'mon, sleepyhead," Mr. Long laughed, pushing her curtains open even wider. "You want me to go up with you?"

"No," Faith said, standing up and stretching. "I'll do it. I'll go and sweep the courts *again*."

"That's my girl," Mr. Long said, smiling.

A few minutes later, Faith was walking up the stone road and over the old wooden bridge. She spotted two ducks nestled in the grass next to the creek. They had their bills tucked under their wings and appeared to be asleep. Faith wished *she* was still sleeping.

Dressed in a suit and tie, Doctor Sipe stood at the top of the hill waiting for her.

"Good morning, Doctor Sipe," Faith said with a forced smile.

"Very disappointing," Doctor Sipe sighed, shaking his head at Faith. "These tennis courts look horrible. I thought you were going to sweep them yesterday."

"I did," Faith replied. "Right after your match."

"Doctor Pruitt and I were the last ones here," Doctor Sipe said. "It was dark when we left last night. Nobody played after us."

"I—I swept the courts, Doctor Sipe. I promise," Faith said.

"I'm a busy man," Doctor Sipe said, walking over to his red sports car. "I don't have time for this nonsense every morning. If I ever see the courts look like this when I'm here to play, I'll make sure you're not working here anymore. Understand?"

"Yes, but—" Faith began.

Doctor Sipe held up his hand. He looked as if he wanted to say something. He opened his mouth, but nothing came out. His face began to turn red as a vein bulged on his forehead. Suddenly he turned, hopped in his car, and drove off. Faith watched him drive down the stone road, a cloud of dust trailing behind him.

"He's so weird," Faith muttered. She took a deep breath and headed back up to the tennis courts. Walking around the clay courts for a minute, she looked around at the ball marks that spotted the courts. Whoever had been up here, she thought, sure hit a lot of tennis balls. He or she must have been hitting for hours and hours.

Faith headed toward the fence to get the broom. Then she stopped suddenly.

"Wait a minute," she whispered. She turned and

walked back onto the court. She stooped over, hands on her knees, to get a good look at the marks again. This time her steps were smaller and slower, with more purpose. Occasionally, Faith would stop, stoop down, and run her hand over one of the marks. Then she stood up and looked for another mark to examine. After a few minutes, she realized that the only marks on the court were made by tennis balls. Again, there were no footprints on the clay surface.

Was it Doctor Sipe ruining the courts? If so, how could he have played on them without leaving footprints? If it wasn't Doctor Sipe, who or what else could be making the marks on the tennis courts? Maybe it was the squirrels, Faith smirked.

After sweeping the courts, she walked down to the barn. Inside she found the coffee can filled with corn. Taking a handful, she tossed it into the grass. She waited for a few seconds for the first squirrel to come down from a tree and start eating. She remembered feeding the squirrels the first time she'd met Mr. West. She remembered what he'd told her. *If you look hard enough, you'll find some magic around here.*

Perhaps it was that magic that was marking up the tennis courts, Faith thought.

9

After breakfast, Faith rode her bike to the library. She wanted to pick up some books and sign up for the summer reading program. If she read five books, which she could easily do, the library would give her a free movie ticket.

Chapter Nine

Faith enjoyed the library. It was quiet—like the tennis club. Some days she went there to find a secluded spot to read. Other times she just sat and thought about things. Today was a thinking day. Faith was content to sit on one of the library's fluffy couches, surrounded by shelves of books, and let her mind wander.

"Have you signed up yet?" a voice asked her.

"What?" Faith asked. She turned to see a young woman putting books away. She paused, smiled at Faith, and then rearranged some books on the shelf. She had long, curly red hair that flowed over her shoulders. When she put the last books away, the woman walked over to Faith.

"Did you sign up?" she asked again. "You know—for the summer reading program." She looked at Faith with big blue eyes and grinned. "It'll be fun. I promise."

"I haven't yet, but I planned to," Faith replied.

"Why don't you do it now?" the young woman asked. "I'll help you."

Faith followed the woman back to her desk. The woman sat down and began shuffling through a pile of papers. Faith spotted the nameplate on the desk that read "Miss Maple."

Miss Maple slid a piece of paper and a pencil across the desk to Faith. She leaned her head to one side and studied Faith.

"I don't remember seeing you around here before. Are you new here?"

"I'm staying with my dad for the summer," Faith replied, taking the pencil and paper. She began to fill out the form for the reading program.

"What's your name?"

"Faith Long."

"Well, Faith Long, I'm Katelyn Maple. What kind of books do you like to read?" she asked.

"Mysteries," Faith said, thinking about the marks on the tennis court.

"When we're done here, I'll show you where to find the mystery books," Miss Maple offered.

"Thanks," Faith said.

Faith picked out a few mysteries and began reading one. After an hour, she decided she'd better head home. She got home just in time for a late lunch.

Her dad had spent most of the morning doing yardwork. He'd also put a final coat of paint on the front porch. Over hamburgers and baked beans, he gave Faith a detailed rundown of his morning's activities. Faith nodded and smiled at all the right times, but in her mind, she was counting the hours till sundown.

●　●　●　●　●

Faith decided to wait until it was totally dark to

sweep the courts. That way, she thought she might catch anyone who was sneaking onto the courts after she cleaned them. She waited until she heard the familiar sound of her dad snoring in front of the TV. Then she slipped on her tennis shoes and quietly tiptoed down the steps and out the front door.

Stepping into the street, she headed for the tennis club. A full moon lit up the sky. The pale moonlight was so bright, Faith could see her own shadow on the ground. The only sound she heard was the crunching of her own shoes. Not even a bird was making a sound. When she reached the old wooden bridge, Faith heard the familiar sound of the creek softly gurgling over the rocks.

About halfway across the bridge, she heard a new sound. POP! POP! POP! Faith looked to the top of the hill and knew instantly where the sound was coming from. She sprinted up the hill, beyond the barn, and up the dirt path to the tennis courts. The tennis court lights weren't on. But she knew someone was hitting tennis balls anyway.

When Faith reached the end of the path, she stopped in her tracks. A man wearing a short-sleeved shirt and dark tennis shorts stood on the court. He was tall and slender with short black hair. His dark brown skin glowed in the moonlight.

The man held a tennis ball in one hand and a small wooden tennis racket in the other. Faith stood in the back of the court watching him bounce a ball on the court and then hit it with the wooden racket. The ball made a loud "crack" when he hit it. Faith watched the ball barely clear the top of the net and make a large mark in the clay when it hit the court. The man paused for a second. Then he reached into his pocket, pulled out another ball, and smashed it across the net.

The man had a small smile on his face as he hit each ball. Whoever he was, he clearly enjoyed hitting tennis balls by himself in the dark. Who is he? Faith asked herself. Maybe she should call the police or Mr. West. She'd never seen him playing here before.

Faith turned and ran down the path from the tennis courts to the barn. She opened the door and flipped on the switch just inside the door. She looked around and found a switch on one of the walls labeled "tennis courts." Turning on the lights, she jogged back up the hill. When she got to the top, she saw that the man was no longer hitting tennis balls. Instead, he held his racket by his side and stared up at the bright lights shining down on him.

Faith took a step onto the court. As she moved into the light, the man turned and spotted her. He stared at her for a few seconds. His dark eyes made her a little nervous. He didn't smile. It was as if he was studying her, Faith thought.

After a moment, the man turned away, reached

into his pocket, and pulled out another tennis ball. She watched him bounce it on the court and hit it with his racket. This time the ball smacked against the top of the net and fell to the ground. It rolled across the court and stopped just in front of Faith. She reached down, picked up the ball, and walked over to the man. She stopped just in front of him and held up the ball.

"Thank you," the man said softly. He looked at her and then held up his hand. "You can keep it if you want. I have plenty more."

Faith looked at the ball in her hand. She spotted the name SIPE printed on it. Her eyes turned to the stranger, who was pulling another ball from his pocket. He bounced it on the court, took a full swing, and slammed it over the net. The man watched the ball roll to a stop.

He turned to Faith and said, "Thanks for the lights."

"You're welcome," Faith replied. She watched him hit another ball. "Will you be done soon? It's late and I need to clean the courts."

"Of course you do, Faith," the man said. He looked at her and smiled. "I can't begin to tell you how nice it is to finally meet you."

"How do you know my name?" Faith asked. She began to feel nervous again. Who was this stranger? Was he dangerous? Faith backed up a little. If he was going to try to grab her, she'd have a head start.

"I—I'm not sure," the man replied honestly. He put his racket down and scratched his head for a few seconds. Looking up to the night sky, he waited as if he expected an answer to drop from the stars. Then he laughed.

"I'm not quite sure how I even got here," he said finally. "I do know two things though. I'm in Pennsylvania, and I know your name is Faith Long."

"What's your name?" Faith asked.

"Arthur—Arthur Ashe," the man replied.

"Well, Mr. Ashe—" Faith began.

"You can call me Arthur," he interrupted. "A long time ago when the newspapers first wrote about me, they never called me 'Art Ashe' or 'Artie Ashe.' No one ever came up with a fancy nickname for me. They just called me 'Arthur.' Just plain 'Arthur.' So that's what you can call me too."

"Okay," Faith agreed.

Arthur leaned over and picked up his racket. He pulled a ball out of his pocket and walked to the back of the court. She watched him bounce the ball once and smack it over the net. Smiling, Arthur turned to look at Faith.

"You want to hit a ball?" he asked. "You can use my racket if you want."

"No," Faith answered quickly. Reaching down, she rubbed the half-heart charm.

Arthur didn't say a word. He just turned and began hitting balls over the net. Faith took a few steps closer to him, watching him hit each ball. She noticed he was hitting them harder than he had before. Each shot grew louder than the last. Faith thought they sounded like firecrackers. After about a dozen shots, Arthur paused and wiped his brow with his hand.

"I saw you play against those men the other day," Arthur said. "You hit the ball pretty hard. Not too many people can hit a tennis ball like that."

"Thanks," Faith said. She took a step toward Arthur. "You said the newspapers didn't give you a nickname. Why were they writing about you?"

"I used to be a pretty good tennis player too," Arthur replied. He wound up and hit a ball over the net. Glancing down at the court, he said, "I won my first big tournament on grass tennis courts. I used to love to play on grass courts. Ever play on grass?"

"No," Faith said.

"They keep the grass cut as short as possible," Arthur explained. "When I'd step onto a grass court, it was like magic. The smell . . . The feel . . . It was like floating on air when I played. You ever feel that way on a tennis court?"

"Not really, Mr. Ashe." Faith shrugged.

"Arthur," he reminded her.

"Okay . . . *Arthur*." Faith corrected, "*These* courts are made of clay. And I'm supposed to sweep them every evening. Now I'm getting in trouble because you're playing here at night."

"What kind of trouble?" Arthur asked.

"People come here to play in the morning," Faith explained. "When they see the courts have ball marks on them, they think I forgot to sweep them. Does Mr. West know you play this late?"

"I doubt it," Arthur said thoughtfully. "It's been a long time since I stepped onto a tennis court. But I like it up here at night. It's quiet and peaceful. No one's around. It's just me, the moon, and the stars.

"You like being alone? Is that why you play so late?" Faith asked.

"It's the only time I *can* play," Arthur explained. "And only on *these* courts.

"I love tennis," he continued. "It's been so long since I've played. Coming here—well, it feels like heaven to me. I couldn't have been sent to a better place."

"Sent?" Faith asked. "Who sent you?"

"I—I'm not sure," Arthur said. "I just know it's been a long time since I've picked up a racket. Back in the 1960s and 1970s, I was one of the best tennis players around. Some days I felt like I could beat anyone. Tennis was my life."

"1960s?" Faith asked. He didn't look old enough

to have been playing in the 1960s. What was up with this guy? Faith stared at the ground, wondering what to say next.

As she studied the ground, Faith noticed that he wasn't making any footprints on the court. He was definitely the one who'd been playing here at night. But how did he do it? She mustered up her courage and asked, "How come you don't leave footprints on the court? Are you a ghost or something?" She said the last part lightly—she didn't really think he was a ghost.

But Arthur responded seriously. "I'll tell you tomorrow—*if* you bring your racket and hit with me."

"Will you give me a hint?" Faith asked.

"Tomorrow," Arthur said and smiled. He pulled a tennis ball out and bounced it on the court. "Come back tomorrow night—and don't forget your racket. If you hit with me, we'll talk."

"How do I know it's safe?" Faith asked. "I don't know who you are or where you came from."

"Go to the library," Arthur suggested. "Look me up! They wrote a bunch of books about me. Now you'd better get going. Your parents are gonna be worried."

"My dad!" Faith blurted out. She knew he'd be worried if he woke up and she still wasn't back. And she still had to sweep the courts! Quickly, she grabbed the broom from the fence. When she turned around, Arthur Ashe was gone and the courts were perfect. All the marks seemed to have vanished.

"Arthur?" Faith called out. Only the chirps of the crickets and the hoot of an owl answered her call. She put the broom back on the fence. Then she ran down to the barn, turned off the court lights, and sprinted home. Glancing over her shoulder only once, she couldn't tell if Arthur was back on the courts or not. All she saw was darkness.

Faith looked up and saw a cloud drifting in front of the moon. The silver moonlight rode along the edges of the cloud. She stopped for a second, looked back, and gazed into the darkness. The barn looked like a big black box now. She couldn't even see the courts anymore. More importantly, she didn't hear the "pop" of tennis balls being hit.

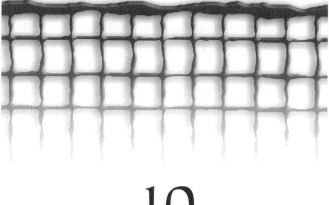

10

Faith was up early the next morning. She couldn't stop thinking about Arthur. Dressing quickly, she jogged down the stairs.

She'd been lucky last night. Her dad had still been asleep when she'd slipped in the door. Since he hadn't said anything when she woke him, she assumed he hadn't realized she'd just gotten home.

"Morning," Mr. Long greeted her now over his paper. "I'm thinking about going to the mall this afternoon. Wanna come along?"

"Not really," Faith replied.

Mr. Long slowly put his paper down on the kitchen table. He looked at Faith with a grin on his face. "Faith Long doesn't want to go shopping? You must have some big plans to pass up a trip to the mall."

"I signed up for the library's summer reading program," Faith explained. She grabbed a muffin off the counter and began to eat it. "I get a free movie pass if I finish it."

"Well, that might be worth missing a trip to the mall," he said, smiling. "Good luck."

"Thanks," Faith said, taking a nibble out of her muffin and heading for the door.

"Got in a little late last night, didn't you?" Mr. Long asked quietly.

Faith froze at the door. She spun around and bit her lower lip. "I—I was at the club," she explained. "I had to wait for someone to finish playing so I could sweep the courts."

"I don't like you staying out so late," Mr. Long said. "Maybe you should sweep the courts in the morning instead."

"Then I'd have to get up really early, Dad. What's the point of being on vacation if I have to get up at the crack of dawn?" Faith looked horrified at the thought.

"Getting up early won't kill you," her dad pointed out. "Lots of us do it and survive."

"I'll be fine, Dad," Faith pleaded her case. "It's only a block away."

"Just try to be home earlier tonight," Mr. Long suggested.

"I will," Faith sighed with a roll of her eyes

as she walked out the door. Immediately tuning out her dad's concerns, she turned her thoughts to Arthur. Who was he? Faith rolled the question around in her mind. Was he real? Was he just kidding with her? Had she imagined the whole thing? By the time she arrived at the library, she was determined to find out the truth.

Faith wasn't sure exactly where to find a book on Arthur. What would it be under? Tennis? Sports? Faith decided to check out the shelves that contained sports books. She scanned the books on the shelf, looking for Arthur's name.

Unsuccessful, she decided to skim through the few books on tennis. It was worth a shot, she thought to herself. Glancing through the books, Faith realized that they wouldn't be much help. They were more about the history of the game or how to play tennis. They didn't really talk about any of the people who played the sport.

"Where are you, Arthur?" Faith asked, closing one of the books. She looked around the room again, this time noticing a set of encyclopedias. Grabbing the first A book she could find, she looked up the name *Ashe*.

"Yes!" she whispered triumphantly. She sat down at a table and began to read.

Arthur Ashe was born and raised in Virginia during the time of the Civil Rights movement. He had played tennis in college and later became a professional tennis player. In 1968, he became the first black man to win the United States Tennis Championship. A few years later, he traveled to England and won their country's greatest tournament, Wimbledon. Yet, for all of his victories, Arthur's life had been a hard one. He'd had two operations on his heart and surgery on his brain. Then he contracted the AIDS virus from a blood transfusion. After that, he'd dedicated his life to fighting for the rights of others until his death in 1993.

"Death?" Faith said to herself. She stared down at the book, reading the last sentence over and over again. So Arthur Ashe was indeed dead. She looked at the picture next to the article. The face looked exactly like the one she'd seen at the club. There was no doubt about it, Faith thought, she'd been talking to a ghost.

Faith imagined what her guidance counselor at school would say if Faith told her about this. Forget about being depressed, she would go straight to crazy.

"I've been talking to a dead guy," Faith mumbled to herself. She slammed the book shut and shoved it back on the shelf. The air around her smelled stale.

She needed a breath of fresh air.

"Faith?" a voice asked. Faith turned to see Miss Maple standing next to a shelf putting books away. "How are you today? Looking for a book to start your reading program?"

"Kinda," Faith replied.

"Well, if I can help you, let me know," Miss Maple offered.

"Thanks, but I have to go," Faith mumbled. She hurried past Miss Maple, almost bumping into her on the way out. Faith walked as fast as she could till she got outside. She stood under a tree, taking deep breaths and trying to relax.

Resting in the tree's shade, Faith formed a plan. She would show up and meet Arthur tonight. And she'd demand to know what was going on. She needed some kind of proof that she wasn't going insane. She wanted proof that she really was seeing the ghost of Arthur Ashe.

11

"Do you believe in ghosts?"

Faith's question hung in the air for a few seconds. Mr. Long tilted his head with a confused look on his face. He took a bite from his peanut butter sandwich and considered Faith's question.

"Ghosts?" he repeated.

"Yeah, Dad, ghosts. Do you believe in them?"

"I—uh—I've never seen—I don't know—Why do you—" Mr. Long stuttered.

"Just curious," Faith said. She gobbled down her ham and cheese sandwich while she thought of the right way to approach her question. "It's just that working around that old barn gives me the creeps. It's pretty old—and I hear noises sometimes."

"Probably just some mice," her dad explained. "I've never seen a ghost, so I guess I don't think they're real. I think it's just that you're up there when it's getting dark and the noises are making your imagination run wild. Why don't you just get up early and sweep the courts in the morning? Okay?"

"Yeah, okay, fine," Faith muttered. "I'll talk to Mr. West tomorrow." How did her question about ghosts end with her having to get up early? she asked herself. Now her whole summer was ruined.

"Good," her dad said, smiling. "By the way, I was trimming around the yard, and I found that tennis ball you lost. Remember? The one you dropped under the porch."

"You found it?" Faith said, amazed at the news.

"Yeah, it was tangled in some weeds," her dad explained.

"Where is it?" Faith asked.

"On the porch," Mr. Long said.

No sooner did Mr. Long finish the sentence than Faith bolted from her chair and out the door. To her right, she saw a pile of weeds, her dad's work gloves, and some gardening tools. She went over and dug through the weeds but couldn't find the tennis ball. She looked around and spotted it under the gloves.

"There you are," Faith said as she snatched up the ball. She rolled it in her hands. Small pieces of clay fell into her hand and onto her father's freshly painted white porch. It looked as if the ball had just been used. Faith brushed the clay off the porch. She examined the ball again and found the name SIPE printed on it. Suddenly, the letters began to change. She held the ball close to her face and watched in amazement as the curves and lines of the red letters began to move. Some of the letters changed and others just faded away. She'd never seen anything like it. In a few seconds, the change was complete. The name SIPE was gone. A new name was now on the ball.

"ASHE," Faith read aloud. She stuck the ball into her pocket. Now she knew she had to go looking for Arthur tonight. He had a lot of explaining to do.

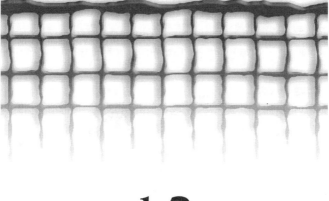

12

When she got to the club that evening, Faith immediately recognized the sound of tennis balls being hit. She paused for a second and looked down at the racket in her hand. Did she really want to go through with this? She thought about it for a moment longer and then continued her sprint up to the courts. Maybe hitting tennis balls with a ghost didn't really count as playing tennis.

"Hello, Faith!" she heard Arthur Ashe call out. He was dressed in the same short-sleeved shirt and dark tennis shorts that he'd worn last night. Faith stood at the entrance to the courts and stared at him. He walked to the edge of the courts and stopped where the grass began. He smiled at Faith and pointed.

"I see you brought your racket. Did you come to play?" Arthur asked.

"Are you a ghost?" Faith blurted out.

"Tell you what," Arthur said with a friendly smile. "You hit some tennis balls to me, and I'll answer some of your questions. Sound fair?"

"I guess so," Faith said and shrugged. She took a deep breath and followed him onto the court.

"Wonderful," Arthur said. He handed Faith two tennis balls, and she ran over to the other side of the court.

"I can't stay very long, Mr. Ashe," Faith warned.

"Arthur," he reminded her.

"It's getting dark—*Arthur*. I can't stay very long."

"That's fine," Arthur said. "We'll just play for a few minutes. I can't tell you how nice it is looking at someone on the other side of a tennis court. It's great to have someone to hit the ball to."

He dropped a ball next to him. Swinging at it with his racket, he hit the ball high and soft. It went right to Faith. The ball bounced high in the air. Faith took a few steps backward and hit the ball back across the net. Arthur returned the ball lower and harder. Running to swing at the shot, Faith missed the ball completely.

"Sorry!" Arthur called out. "Just had to see if I could still hit it hard."

"It's okay," Faith replied. They played for a few more minutes. Faith noticed that Arthur ran around the tennis court with great ease. He didn't look as if he were trying to run fast, but he got to every ball she hit. His long legs and arms made it easy for him to reach every shot. Faith noticed that Arthur was smiling the entire time they played.

"Okay!" Faith called out, holding her racket in the air. "Wait a minute. You said you'd answer some of my questions."

"All right," Arthur replied. "A deal's a deal. Go ahead. What's on your mind?"

"Why don't your feet make marks on the court?" Faith asked. She pointed down at his tennis shoes. "I've been watching your feet. It's like they don't touch the ground."

"Good footwork," Arthur explained. He raised his finger and pointed at Faith. "If you stay on your toes and take small steps, you'll move like the wind too."

"I don't know," Faith said in disbelief. "I think there's something else to it."

"Sounds like another question," Arthur said, raising his eyebrows.

"I did what you said," Faith told him. "I went to the library and looked you up. If you're really Arthur Ashe, then you're dead. Does that mean you're a ghost?"

"It means I'm Arthur Ashe," he said simply. "And I've been sent here to help you."

"Help me?" Faith asked, confused. "With what?"

"To find something you lost," Arthur explained.

"Like what?"

"Let's hit some more," Arthur suggested, ignoring her question. He turned and walked to the back of the court. He lobbed the ball over the net to Faith. They volleyed for a few more minutes. Faith felt strange hitting a tennis ball again. She enjoyed playing with Arthur even though he was a much better player. Faith recalled that when she hit with people who were better, she played better too. This was one of those times.

But now the light was growing dim. The full moon was lingering on the horizon. Stars began to appear in the crimson-colored sky. It was starting to get difficult to see Arthur standing in the shadows. The balls were becoming almost impossible to return.

"Stop!" Faith called out. She walked up to the net. "It's getting late, and I have to sweep the courts before I go home."

"Okay," Arthur said. "Thank you. This is the best I've felt in a long time. Coming out here. Feeling the air in my lungs. The clay under my feet. Even the sound the racket makes when I swing it through the air. I feel so alive."

"So," Faith hesitated before asking the question, "are you dead then?"

"Would it scare you if I was?"

"I don't know," Faith answered honestly. "I guess

not. It would just be weird. But you seem nice and all."

"I've always believed that treating people with respect and kindness helps to bridge any barriers. Whether it's skin color, age, or money. If you treat people nicely, all that other stuff doesn't matter."

"So even though you're dead and I'm alive, you think we can still be friends?"

"Death is a great divider," Arthur explained, "but sometimes you can work around it. I'd like to play here a few more evenings—and I'd like you to hit with me. I'd be honored to call you a friend."

Faith took down the brush from the fence and began to clean the court. Arthur followed beside her while she swept. She didn't answer his invitation. She'd made a choice not to play tennis again, and she was determined to stick to that decision.

"So what do you say, Faith?" Arthur asked again. "Can you come up again? Come and hit with me?"

"I—I can't," Faith replied finally, keeping her head down while she swept the courts.

"I see," Arthur said quietly. He dropped his racket on the court and continued to walk beside Faith. "I thought you were having fun tonight?"

"It's not that. It's just that I—I stopped playing a while ago," Faith explained. "I made a promise to myself to stop playing. I want to keep that promise. Did you ever make a promise to yourself, Arthur?"

"Oh, yes," Arthur said and smiled. "Sometimes the hardest promises to keep are the ones we make to ourselves."

"Well, I've already broken my promise twice this week," Faith said. She stopped sweeping and turned to Arthur. "I can't do it again, so I can't play with you."

"I understand," Arthur said. He looked down at her and rubbed the back of his neck. "Would it be okay if I brought someone else to play with me?"

"Sure, I guess." Faith shrugged. "I'm gonna start coming up early in the mornings to sweep the courts, so if you want to play at night, I guess that's okay."

"Are you *sure* you don't want to play some more? It's a beautiful night."

"Pretty sure." Faith nodded.

"Okay then, I'm not going to push you," Arthur said. "It's your decision."

He turned and began to walk toward the other court. Faith watched him quietly move into the shadows that stretched across the court. A few seconds later, Arthur walked into the darkness and vanished into nothing

"Wow!" Faith said. She put down the brush and ran across the court. All that remained was a tennis ball with the name ASHE on it. Faith picked up the ball and just stared at it for a long moment. Finally, she set the ball near her racket and finished sweeping the courts. When she was done, Faith picked up the ball and her racket and headed toward home.

When she reached her house, Faith saw her dad sitting on a chair on the front porch. He waved to Faith as she walked across the front yard.

"Hey, kiddo," her dad said. He pointed to the racket in her hand. "You sneaking out to play some tennis?" He smiled broadly.

"I—uh—" Faith stammered. She looked down at her racket and then back at her dad's smiling face. "I just took it up to the club. Thought I might want to hit some by myself—but I didn't. While I was there, I swept the courts. I'll start doing it in the mornings after this." It was the best excuse she could think of. And, she told herself, she wasn't really lying to her dad. She hadn't played alone. She had hit some balls with Arthur Ashe. Her dad wouldn't have believed *that* even if she'd told him.

"Okay, that's fine," her dad said.

Walking onto the porch, Faith sat down next to her dad. She pulled the racket onto her lap and stared at it.

"Dad," Faith began, "would you love me more if I played tennis?"

"What?" Mr. Long asked.

"If I played tennis," Faith said. She took a deep breath and tried to relax. "Would you love me more if I played again?"

"Oh, honey," Mr. Long sighed. He put his arm around her shoulder and pulled her close to him. "I love you more than I love anything or anyone. It doesn't matter to me if you play tennis or not. I just want you to be happy."

"So you don't care if I play?" Faith persisted.

"Like I said," her dad repeated, "I just want you to be happy. I thought tennis made you happy. You used to smile and laugh a lot. Especially with that one girl—the one from Florida. What was her name?"

"Meredith," Faith replied. She looked down at the half of a heart that was dangling from her neck.

"Yeah—Meredith," Mr. Long said. "You two were inseparable for a while. Now, I don't even think you two keep in touch anymore. What happened? I know you miss her. And the tennis seemed to bring you two together."

"And push us apart," Faith added.

"I know." Mr. Long nodded. "But I thought you'd be able to get past that. I guess not."

Mr. Long squeezed his daughter's shoulders tightly. Together they sat and looked out at the night. The moon was higher in the sky but as bright as the previous night. Faith lowered her head and rested it on her dad's shoulder. She felt warm and safe sitting with him.

"You know it wasn't your fault," Mr. Long pointed out, breaking the silence. "Sometimes things happen.

What happened to Meredith wasn't because of you."

"I know," Faith mumbled. She said the words more for her dad than for herself. She knew that what had happened to Meredith *was* her fault. Winning that tennis match had caused something terrible to happen to a friend. She couldn't forget it— and she couldn't play again. Not even with Arthur Ashe.

"Faith?" Mr. Long said. He'd been watching her and noticing how she was just staring straight ahead without blinking. She looked lost in her memories and emotions.

"Are you okay?" he asked her.

"Yeah, Dad," Faith said with a quick smile. "I'm fine." She stood up and twirled the racket in her hand. "Just tired, I guess. I'm gonna go to bed."

"Sweet dreams," Mr. Long told her. "By the way, Mom's gonna call tomorrow morning. She wants to hear about your job."

"Okay."

In her room, Faith opened her closet door and put her racket away. She started to close the door but then paused and looked inside. Her eyes drifted to the back of the closet and stopped when she spotted the box that held her trophies. She stared at the box for a few seconds. Then she closed the door slowly and got ready for bed.

13

Since she had cleaned the courts the night before, Faith slept in the next morning. After speaking with her mom, she rode her bike to the library.

Miss Maple spotted Faith as soon as she walked through the front door.

"Faith!" she called out with excitement in her voice. "Can you come with me? I have something I want to show you."

"Okay," Faith managed to say as Miss Maple grabbed her hand and pulled her along to her desk.

"Someone was looking in a tennis magazine, and she found this picture," Miss Maple said, handing Faith a magazine. "Is that you?"

Faith looked at the black and white photo of herself hitting a tennis ball. The caption under her picture read, "Faith Long Becomes the National Champion."

Faith handed the magazine back to Miss Maple. "Yes, that's me," Faith said.

"Oh, Faith!" Miss Maple laughed. "This is fantastic! Maybe you could speak with some of our younger readers. I mean, a tennis champion like you, they'll listen to what you say."

"I don't want—What would I—I wouldn't know what to say," Faith stammered.

"Well," Miss Maple began, "this magazine says you're the best tennis player in the country in your age group. Some people might want to know what that feels like."

"Trust me, they don't want to know what it feels like," Faith said.

Ignoring Faith's comment, Miss Maple gushed, "You must feel so special. I think it's just wonderful that we have a tennis champion in our little town. You think about it and let me know when you could talk with the kids."

"I'm sorry, Miss Maple," Faith apologized. "I don't want to do it. I'm sorry."

"But—" Miss Maple started to say. Before she could finish, Faith turned and walked away.

Trying to escape Miss Maple, Faith dropped down on to one of the couches far away from the librarian's desk. She felt bad about not being able to help Miss Maple, but she just wasn't ready to talk about that day. That day, she'd won the most important tennis match of her life. For a brief moment, she'd been thrilled. Not only had she won the title, but she'd made both of her parents happy. It was the last time she'd seen them kiss each other. It was also the last time their family was together the way Faith thought all families should be. And it was the last time she and Meredith were together . . .

Faith shook herself back to the present. "Arthur," she whispered aloud. "I need to find out more about you."

Heading to the nonfiction section, Faith spotted the biographies. Now that she knew Arthur really had been a famous tennis player, she thought maybe the library would have a biography about him. Still, she was kind of surprised when she actually found a book on him. Pulling the book from the shelf, Faith sat down and began to read.

Arthur had taken a trip to South Africa. It was a place where black people didn't have the same rights as white people. Some people were angry about Arthur's trip. They said he'd only do more harm than good by going. But Arthur hadn't listened. He'd wanted to see for himself how badly the people were suffering. He also wanted to inspire them—be a role model for them. On his trip, Arthur tried to make the black people realize that they could do whatever they dreamed of doing, including fighting racial barriers.

Faith spent most of the morning and part of the afternoon curled up with the book on Arthur. It was her stomach that reminded her of the time. Since she was visiting for the summer and didn't have a library card, Faith returned the book to the shelf.

Leaving the library quickly, Faith headed home. As she coasted through the streets, she wondered if she should stop at the tennis club on her way home. In the end, she decided against it. If Arthur was there, she would just be tempted to play tennis again.

● ● ● ● ●

Lying in her bed that night, Faith continued to think about the tennis club. She looked at the open curtains waving slightly in the summer breeze. She'd left them open tonight because she wanted to get up early in the morning. She was going to try sweeping the courts in the morning like her dad had suggested. The sunlight streaming through her window was sure to wake her.

Yet, even knowing that she had to get up early, Faith was having trouble getting to sleep. She turned over. She pulled her sheet up to her neck. Then she got hot, so she pushed the sheet back down. Staring across the room, Faith watched as the moonlight splashed against her window. Finally, she got out of bed and went over to the window. The cool night air flowed over her.

"Gotta get to sleep," Faith mumbled to herself. She turned her head, and the wind played with her hair. The moon and stars burned brightly against the dark night sky.

Suddenly Faith remembered that Arthur had asked if he could bring someone else to hit with him tonight. Faith was curious about who Arthur was playing against. Was it another ghost?

Faith had to know. She pulled on some clothes and shoes and then slipped downstairs and into the night.

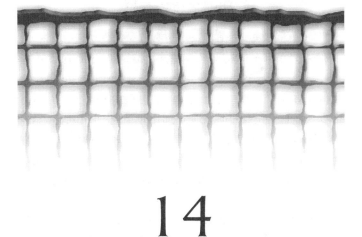

14

As Faith walked down the street, the sound of tennis balls grew louder. She found herself walking faster. The moon provided enough light for her to follow the road to the bridge. Crossing it, she squinted and tried to look up the hill at the tennis courts.

POP! POP! POP! The sounds were even louder and closer together now. Suddenly Faith found herself sprinting up the hill to the courts. She stopped when she saw Arthur there. He was running to meet a ball.

Faith looked to the other side of the court. A woman wearing a white dress and a long white scarf around her neck was returning Arthur's hit. Her dress rippled when she moved. Her scarf fluttered behind her with each step. How can she play in that? Faith wondered, noting how the woman's dress fell below her knees. Faith couldn't imagine playing tennis in a dress. She hated wearing dresses to begin with, but play tennis in one?

Faith watched the woman move around the court taking small steps like a dancer. As the ball came to her, she took a loose, easy swing at it. The ball shot off her racket with a loud crack.

"Wait!" the woman called out and sprinted to the side of the court. She bent down and picked up a green leaf that had fallen from one of the trees. She carefully touched the leaf with her fingers and then held it to her nose and smelled it. She laughed and rubbed the leaf against her cheek.

"It's just as I remember, Arthur. Isn't it wonderful here?"

"Yes, it is," Arthur shouted back. He walked around the back of the court and spotted Faith.

"Hello, Faith!" he called. "Come here. I have someone I'd like you to meet."

Arthur walked up to the net at the center of the court, waving Faith over to him. When she reached him, Faith noticed the woman at the other end of the court was walking toward them. She was tall and thin, with dark hair and bright red lipstick. She smiled at Faith, revealing a row of crooked teeth.

"Faith," Arthur said, pointing to the woman, "this is Suzanne Lenglen. She's one of the greatest tennis players in the history of France."

"Nice to meet you!" Faith said, turning to Miss Lenglen.

"Such a sweet girl," Miss Lenglen said, taking

Faith's hand in her own. Miss Lenglen's hand felt cold to Faith, and she thought about pulling away. Miss Lenglen seemed to sense this and let go of Faith's hand.

"Thank you for letting me come here to play, my dear," Miss Lenglen said. "It's been so long since I've seen clay courts like these. The feel of French clay under my feet again is wonderful. It's just all so lovely."

"Yes, it is," Faith replied, a bit confused. "When did you play tennis, Miss Lenglen?"

"Way back in the 1920s," Miss Lenglen recalled, fixing her hair. "No one could beat me back then. I was the best in all the world. There's nothing quite like the feeling of knowing you're better than everyone else at something."

"I wouldn't know." Faith shrugged.

"That's not what Arthur tells me." Miss Lenglen grinned with her bright red lips.

"Suzanne!" Arthur scolded.

"Come now, Arthur," Miss Lenglen said. "Not only is she a beautiful child, but she's a wonderful tennis player. It's all so clear. She could be a champion. All she needs is a spark."

"A what?" Faith asked.

"A spark. A fire," Miss Lenglen explained. "Something that makes you want to go out on a tennis court and play the best you can. You see, my dear, every champion has a secret. Would you like to know mine?"

"Sure," Faith replied.

"To be the best," Miss Lenglen shared, "you can't worry about who you play against. You only worry about playing the best you can. If you play your best, Faith, I promise that you'll win a lot of matches."

"No," Faith disagreed, "there's more to it than that. Winning isn't just about doing your best. It's about beating someone else and making her feel bad. Sometimes it even changes her life."

"But—" Arthur began.

"Nonsense!" Miss Lenglen interrupted. She pointed her racket at Faith. "I've lost more tennis matches in my life than a lot of people. Sure it hurt sometimes, but I kept playing. Whoever you beat will live to play another match."

"Not always," Faith said quietly.

Miss Lenglen simply smiled at Faith and shook her head. She looked down at Faith and gazed deeply into her eyes. Faith could feel her legs tingle.

"She needs a spark, Arthur!" Miss Lenglen observed again. She continued to stare at Faith, studying her face as she had the leaf.

"Her eyes are dark and empty. She needs a spark—it's just that simple."

"Yes, Suzanne," Arthur agreed. "I know."

"Now let's play!" Miss Lenglen called out, walking to the back of the court.

"In a minute," Arthur said, raising his finger in the air. Miss Lenglen began to collect some of the tennis balls that were scattered around the court.

"Don't mind her," Arthur told Faith. "She always says what's on her mind. I always wished I could have been more like that."

"Me too," Faith said. She thought about what he'd said for a moment and then frowned.

"What's wrong?" Arthur asked.

"Well, I don't understand why you were afraid to say what you thought," Faith explained. "I mean, I'm a kid. If I say what I think, my mom or my teachers would yell at me. But you are—I mean *were*—an adult. You were famous. Why couldn't you say what you wanted? People would have listened to you."

"Oh, I'm sure they would have listened," Arthur said, shaking his head. He looked at Faith and sighed. "But would they have understood? When a lot of people are listening, it's important to say the right thing. But sometimes it's hard to know what that is. You have to choose your words carefully."

"Arthur!" Miss Lenglen shouted from across the court. "Let's play!"

"All right!" Arthur called back. He looked at Faith. "Stay and play with us. You can use my racket. It'll be fun."

Faith looked at Arthur. He held out his racket. Faith looked around and saw Miss Lenglen watching them. Part of her wanted to take it, but she found herself taking a small step backward instead.

"I'm sorry," Faith sighed.

"It's okay," Arthur replied. "Maybe you can stay and watch a little."

"I have to go."

"But I'll only be here two more nights," Arthur told her.

"Why?" Faith asked.

"I told you before that I could only be here for a few nights," Arthur reminded her. "After that, I have to go."

"Oh," Faith said, feeling sad. She liked Arthur. He seemed like a nice man, even if he *was* dead. Something about him made Faith feel comfortable. He didn't talk to her as if she were a child. He listened to what she said and seemed to really care. It was strange, Faith thought, but the club wouldn't feel the same without Arthur around.

"Okay, Suzanne, I'm ready," Arthur called out, jogging onto the court.

"Finally!" Suzanne grumbled and hit a ball over to Arthur. "It's not like I have all night! We only have a few hours. Let's play!"

Faith watched Arthur smash a shot so hard that Miss Lenglen didn't even try to run for it. Without hesitating, Arthur reached into his pocket, pulled out another ball, and hit it to her. Faith stayed for a minute and then quietly turned and walked away.

On the walk home, Faith looked up at the stars and thought about Miss Lenglen's words. She thought Faith was missing a spark. What had she meant by that? Faith wasn't feeling as down as she had during school. She'd actually been feeling a little better lately, especially with Arthur around.

"No spark," Faith murmured, crossing the bridge.

Dear Meredith,

Sometimes late at night, I dream about the last time we played tennis together. I dream about how much I made you run and how your leg was bothering you. And I dream about winning the match, shaking your hand, and watching you cry. I wish I had known why. Now I know and I wish I hadn't won at all.

Faith

15

Faith woke early the next morning. The bright sunlight made her squint as she rolled out of bed. She fumbled through her drawers, half awake, till she found a pair of shorts and a T-shirt to wear. She let out a long yawn while she got dressed.

Next, Faith went downstairs and grabbed a glass of orange juice. The tangy taste helped her wake up a little more. Swallowing the last of it, she put the glass in the sink and headed out the door.

"Morning," Mr. Long greeted. He was digging in the yard when he spotted her. He brushed the dirt from his hands.

"I'm going to sweep the tennis courts," Faith said, yawning.

"Good." Mr. Long nodded. "Will you be home right after?"

"I was thinking about going to the library afterward," Faith replied.

"Okay, I'm gonna run into town and pick up a bush to plant here," Mr. Long said. "So I might not be here when you get back. Maybe I'll see you for lunch?"

"Sure." Faith shrugged.

"Say hi to Mr. West for me."

"I will," Faith said, walking out to the street. She hoped she'd get to the courts before anyone else. It was a weekday, and she knew that most of the club members would be working. She quickened her pace anyway just to be sure. She didn't want to get in trouble again.

When she crossed the bridge, her worry turned into panic when she spotted two cars parked in front of the barn. Faith took off in a full jog up the hill to the tennis courts. When she reached the courts, she found the Nortons hitting to each other and Mr. West sitting on a chair next to the courts watching the brothers play.

"Hello, Faith!" one Norton called out.

"Hello, Faith!" the other Norton repeated.

"Hi!" Faith grinned and waved. She walked over to where Mr. West was sitting and pulled up a chair beside him. "Morning, Mr. West."

"Morning, Faith," Mr. West replied. "The courts looked beautiful this morning."

"They did?" Faith asked, a little surprised. "I mean—thank you."

"Mornings like this are made for tennis. Sam and Stan are lucky to be out there," Mr. West said wistfully.

"Did they take off from work?" Faith asked.

"They play every Thursday morning," Mr. West said. "I guess they just go into the office a little late. Since they own their own firm, they don't have to worry about getting in trouble with the boss."

Faith just nodded. She turned to see Mr. West watching the brothers' shots. His eyes grew wide at some of the better shots. He grimaced at a few of the others. Sometimes he'd rock in his seat as if he were ready to jump up. Just as Arthur smiled while he played the game, Mr. West seemed happy just to be close to it.

Faith turned just in time to see one Norton hit a low, hard shot that his brother couldn't reach.

"Nice shot, Sam!" Mr. West shouted and clapped.

"Do you still play tennis?" Faith asked Mr. West.

"I wish I could," Mr. West replied. "My doctor told me not to—at least not competitively. Sometimes, though, I'll sneak out and hit a couple by myself, but it's not the same as playing. I used to love to play against anyone."

"Why did you love it?" Faith asked.

"What's that, Faith?" Mr. West asked, his head turning from side to side as he watched the ball go back and forth.

"Nothing," Faith mumbled quietly. After one long exchange that ended with Sam Norton hitting the ball into the net, the Nortons jogged over to Mr. West and Faith. Both Nortons were smiling from ear to ear. They were breathing hard, and their round bellies looked like two balloons inflating and deflating.

"The courts are great." Sam grinned.

"You're doing a wonderful job," Stan told Faith.

"Yes, she is," Mr. West agreed. He took out his pipe and began to light it. "You guys looked like you were playing some good points. Who won?"

"We don't keep score," Sam announced.

"Why not?" Faith asked.

"We just like to play," Stan explained. "It's the best way for both of us to have fun. That's the most important thing, don't you think so, Faith?"

"I guess so," Faith said. She hadn't thought about tennis being fun in a long time.

"Maybe you should play with us some morning," Stan suggested.

"That would be splendid," Sam chimed in.

"Yes," Stan agreed, "it would be."

"Simply splendid." Sam nodded. Together the Nortons walked away, discussing how "splendid" it would be to have Faith play with them. Faith thought it was odd how they didn't really ask her whether she'd like to play or not. They just seemed thrilled with the idea.

"Do you miss playing tennis, Faith?" Mr. West asked.

"Not the matches," Faith quickly answered. "Sometimes I think about just going out and hitting by myself though.

"How about you, Mr. West? Do you miss it?" she asked.

"Oh, yes," Mr. West replied without hesitation. "Before I started having health problems, I used to try to play tennis every day during the summer. I always learned something new about the game. I also learned something new about myself whenever I played. Since I stopped playing, I feel like I've lost a friend. And on days like this, I miss my friend."

"I'm sorry," Faith said. She thought hard before deciding to say her next words. "I could bring my racket and hit a few with you some morning."

"That's okay, Faith," Mr. West said, smiling. "I didn't tell you all this for you to feel sorry for me. I just wanted you to understand why I hang around here so much. It's not because I'm an old man with nothing better to do."

"They're also your courts," Faith pointed out.

"Yes." Mr. West nodded. "When I was young, I thought I'd play on these courts forever. I never thought about getting old—or sick. It never occurred to me that someday I wouldn't be able to play. You just don't think about those things when you're young, do you?"

"Guess not," Faith replied.

"Life's funny that way," Mr. West observed. He struggled to his feet and reached into a pants pocket. He pulled out some rolled-up dollar bills. "Anyway," he said, "I was hoping you'd be up here this morning. I owe you some money, don't I?"

"I guess," Faith said, trying to sound uninterested. Inside, her heart was flying when she saw her first two-week's pay in Mr. West's hand. He started flipping through the dollar bills, counting to himself.

"Here you go, Faith," Mr. West said when he stopped counting. He looked at her and laughed at the expression on her face as he handed her the money. "Looks like we found something else you love besides tennis."

"Yes, sir," Faith laughed. "Thank you."

"No," Mr. West said, "I should thank *you*. Everyone's happy with what you've been doing. Keep up the good work."

"I will." Faith grinned. She raced off the court and shot down the hill in a sprint. Today was definitely going to be a day for the mall. She held up the money in her hand as she ran home. Out of breath halfway up the street, Faith began to walk. She wiped the sweat from her forehead and looked at the money one more time to make sure she wasn't just dreaming.

For the first time in a long time, Faith felt almost completely happy—almost. In the back of her mind, she could still hear some of the words that Mr. West had spoken. How he thought of tennis as a friend. How he missed his "friend" now that he couldn't play anymore. It made Faith feel a little sad. She wanted to help Mr. West. She wanted to play tennis with him.

The only problem was that she wasn't playing tennis anymore. She'd made that promise to herself, and she was going to keep it. So far this summer, she'd played one point and hit for a few minutes with a ghost. Could she go further and hit with Mr. West for a while? She wouldn't be playing to win, she justified. No one would get hurt.

Faith wasn't sure what to do. She needed more time to think. Maybe she could even talk to Arthur about it.

16

Faith spent the afternoon shopping at the mall. It was only a ten-minute ride from her house by bike. It felt good spending a hot, sticky summer day in air-conditioned comfort while going from store to store. Some of the money went toward a new pair of sunglasses. Some went to the food court for a soft pretzel since Faith couldn't resist the smell. After purchasing a pair of jeans she'd wanted for a while, she ducked into the music store and picked up a new CD.

She made one last stop at the bookstore. She found a book on the best tennis matches in history. It was a paperback book that only cost a couple dollars. She planned to give it to Mr. West. Even though he couldn't play anymore, Faith thought he might still like to read about tennis on the days no one came to the club. Besides, Faith reasoned, if she wasn't going to play with him, this was the least she could do.

Later in the day, she decided to take the book down to the tennis club. She was excited about giving it to Mr. West.

When she reached the club, Faith found the barn and the courts completely empty. The wind hissed as it slipped through the tree branches and raced down the hill to the creek below. Faith sat in Mr. West's chair and held the book on her lap. Suddenly a ball came bouncing down the path from the tennis courts. It rolled right next to Faith and stopped. She picked it up and found two words printed on the ball. COME HERE.

She couldn't hear anyone playing on the courts. Was it a joke, she thought, or was it Arthur? Faith put the book down on Mr. West's chair and walked up the path to the tennis courts. Stepping onto the courts, she looked around. A chipmunk scurried across one end of the courts, but otherwise they were empty.

Faith remembered watching Arthur and Suzanne play here the previous night. She looked over to the spot where she remembered seeing Suzanne for the first time. Another tennis ball lay in the exact spot. Faith walked over and picked it up. Unlike the last ball, this one had three words printed on it. Faith read them aloud. "TO THE FIELD."

Faith turned and looked at the tall stalks of corn. She started to walk toward the row of corn closest to the courts when a ball popped out from the shadows. It rolled right to where Faith was standing. She picked it up. Again, three words appeared. WE MUST TALK.

Faith carried all three balls with her into the field. She ducked under some giant stalks and pushed aside their large green leaves. She walked for about 20 feet and then turned and looked around.

"Hello!" she called out. The cornstalks stirred in the passing breeze. She spotted a rabbit nibbling on some greens. A crow called out from a nearby tree. Only nature seemed to be responding to her. She looked around again and noticed something on the ground. It was another tennis ball. *COME BACK TONIGHT.*

Faith dropped all the balls on the ground and looked around again. She found one last ball about a foot from where she was standing. When she picked this one up, it had one word printed on it. *ASHE.*

Faith stepped out of the field carrying all five balls and was surprised to see a man standing on one of the courts. Taking a closer look, she realized it was Doctor Sipe.

"What are you—" Faith started to ask and then stopped herself from saying more.

"Just checking on things," Doctor Sipe replied. Dressed in white shorts and a white shirt, he looked as if he were ready to play. Taking off his glasses, he pointed at Faith. "Are those my tennis balls?"

"Uh—no—" Faith mumbled.

"Well, then whose are they?" Doctor Sipe snapped. He walked briskly across the court and stopped in front of Faith. He stared down at her and pointed at the five balls she was holding in her hands.

"They're—ah—mine," Faith answered clumsily.

"Mr. West said you don't play tennis anymore," Doctor Sipe pointed out. His eyebrows lowered and he pressed his lips together. "Are you stealing them?"

"No, Doctor Sipe," Faith replied. "I was—uh— practicing by myself—earlier this morning—and then I came back to sweep the courts."

Doctor Sipe didn't say a word. He held out both of his hands. "Let me see them," he demanded.

Faith handed them to him one at a time. She wondered what Doctor Sipe would say when he read the words on the balls. She held her breath while she watched him examine each one, holding them up as if they were pieces of fruit. After he'd look at one, he'd drop it on the court and look at the next one. When he'd dropped the last ball, he merely glared at her and then walked away.

"Creep," Faith muttered to herself. She picked up one of the balls and turned it in her hand. The words were gone. Faith walked around and picked up the other balls. There were no words on any of them.

But even though the words had vanished, Faith still remembered the message. She knew she had to come back tonight to see Arthur.

17

At sunset, Faith left for the club. Ribbons of golden light fell from the trees that lined the street. When she reached the club, she noticed how the setting sun bathed the land. From treetops to grassy hills, it seemed as if everything had turned to gold. Faith stood on the tennis courts, looked to the sunset, and closed her eyes. She could feel the sunlight strike her face with a warm caress. In her mind, she remembered last summer.

She could see herself standing on a beach in Florida watching the sun set over the ocean with her best friend, Meredith. It was one of her favorite memories from last summer—one of her best memories of Meredith.

When she'd started traveling a lot to play tennis tournaments, Faith had met plenty of girls from all over the country. Some of them wore headsets, listened to music, and kept to themselves. Others carried books or magazines and read while they waited to play their matches. Faith had found it difficult to strike up a conversation or make any friends. Most of the girls just wanted to win their matches and be left alone.

Meredith had been the only one who talked to Faith. She and Faith had hit it off as soon they met at a tournament in Nashville, Tennessee. In the months that followed, Faith and Meredith had been inseparable. Whenever they saw each other at a tournament, the conversation and laughter seemed to pick up where it had left off at the last tournament. They liked the same clothes, the same music, and the same junk food. Eating corn chips and playing cards were two of their favorite ways to kill time between their matches.

Faith reached down and pulled out her necklace from beneath her shirt. She took the half-heart charm between her fingers and rubbed it. Meredith had the other half of the heart. It was a friendship charm, and Faith thought about their friendship every time she wore the necklace. It was because of tennis that she had met Meredith. It was also because of tennis that she had lost Meredith. Faith had caused her best friend more pain than she could ever imagine. More pain than any person should ever have to know. When Faith promised herself not to play tennis, it was also a promise she was making to Meredith. A promise she felt she should keep.

"Good evening, Faith," a soft voice said from behind her.

Faith spun around to see a man sitting on a courtside bench. Long, narrow shadows cast down from the trees made it hard to see who it was. She took a few steps closer and looked into the shadows. It was Arthur. He was holding his tennis racket on his lap, still dressed in the same dark shorts and white tennis shirt.

"You didn't bring your racket," Arthur observed.

"I forgot," Faith lied.

Arthur didn't say a word. He stayed on the bench, sitting in the shadows. She could see him look up at the orange and red swirls in the sky. He sat upright, staring at the sky.

"Isn't it beautiful?" he asked in awe.

Faith looked up at the sky. It seemed like any other sunset to her. When she noticed the smile on Arthur's face, she looked at the sky once more. A pure peach sky was growing into a darker shade of orange along the horizon. It was pretty, but she still felt she wasn't getting Arthur's meaning. Arthur seemed to see something in the sky that she couldn't.

"I'd forgotten how beautiful a sunset could be," Arthur sighed. He stood up and stepped out into the light. The fading rays struck Arthur, and suddenly Faith could see right through him. It was like looking through stained glass, Faith thought. Arthur looked at her. The look on her face must have told him something was wrong. He looked down and noticed where he was. Quickly, he stepped back into the shade.

"The sunset," Faith mumbled, trying not to draw attention to what had happened. "It doesn't look special to me. It looks just like yesterday's sunset."

"I didn't see yesterday's sunset," Arthur pointed out. He looked at Faith and smiled. "But I'll remember this one."

Faith nodded and looked down at her feet. She kicked some clay with the tip of her shoe.

"I saw you over there," Arthur observed. He pointed to where Faith had been standing with her eyes closed. "What were you thinking about?"

"A friend," Faith said quietly. She took a few steps closer to Arthur. "When you played tennis, did you ever hurt someone?"

"Sometimes I'd accidentally hit my opponent with a tennis ball," Arthur recalled.

"That's not what I mean," Faith said. She walked right in front of Arthur and looked up to him. "When you played tennis, did you ever make people angry? Or do things that made them sad?"

"Oh, yes," Arthur began. "When I first started to play tennis, it was hard for me to play in tournaments because of my skin color. Back then, it made some people mad when they saw a black tennis player playing at a club that didn't have any black members. It made them furious if I won. I didn't let it stop me though. So what about you? Do you make people mad when you play tennis?"

"Not exactly," Faith said. She sat down on the bench, folded her arms, and stared down at the court. "I knew this girl. Her name was Meredith. I met her two years ago. We hit it off and became friends. Whenever I'd have to travel to another state for a tournament, Meredith was always there and we'd always hang out. We were best friends."

"Were?" Arthur noted.

"Meredith was a good tennis player," Faith continued, ignoring Arthur's comment, "but she was always hurt. When she'd show up at a tournament, she'd always have a bump over her eye or a bruise on her arm. Meredith always made excuses for her injuries."

Faith took a deep breath and continued. "I played against her one time. It was the finals of a national tournament in Miami, Florida. The winner would be number one for our age group in the whole United States. It was a big deal. Meredith had a sore knee that day and wasn't moving around the court very well. I ran her as much as I could because I wanted to win."

Faith looked up. Arthur just nodded in understanding.

"I could tell her leg was really hurting, but I didn't slow down. I thought she'd quit, but she just kept playing," Faith recalled. She could see the match clearly in her mind. "She was limping around the court, crying between points, but she wouldn't stop playing. When I won, we shook hands. She was crying hard. I thought it was because she lost. I hugged her and told her, 'It'll be okay, Meredith. It'll be fine.' But she just kept crying."

Faith paused. She took another breath and tried to relax.

"Then what happened?" Arthur asked.

"When she let go of my hand, she walked over to get her rackets. Her dad was standing there waiting. He shouted at her and then slapped her across the face. I just stood at the net. I couldn't speak. I watched him point at her and yell as loud as I've ever heard anyone yell. Some parents next to the court started to yell at him, but he just grabbed Meredith and dragged her off the court. I remember Meredith turning and looking at me for a split second as he grabbed her arm. The look in her eyes just . . ."

Faith could feel her eyes start to water. If she tried, she could picture the red mark on Meredith's face from where she'd been slapped.

"And then?" Arthur prodded.

"Meredith didn't play in the next couple of tournaments," Faith said. "I thought maybe her knee was sore and she was taking a break. Then I found out the truth."

"What was it?" Arthur asked quietly.

"Meredith . . ." Faith began. Her voice broke and she started to cry.

"It's okay, Faith," Arthur said.

"Meredith was in the hospital," Faith finished on a sob. "Her dad beat her up. Then he pushed her down some steps and broke her arm. She was in a lot of pain for a long time all because I had to win. He hit her because of me. It was my fault."

Faith's head dipped down and she let out a flood of tears. Sharing her story with someone had released something inside her. She cried for Meredith and for their lost friendship.

"Faith," Arthur finally said softly. He reached out and rubbed her arm. "Is that why you've given up on tennis? Because of Meredith?"

"I—" Faith tried to speak but broke down again. "I just don't want to cause anyone the kind of pain I caused Meredith," she gulped out. "I don't need to win! I don't need to play tennis!"

"Oh, but you do," Arthur corrected quietly.

"No!" Faith cried louder. "No, I don't! I won't!"

"Faith," Arthur said calmly, "I wish I could tell you everything's going to be okay if you give up tennis. But I can't. Life isn't that simple. But I can tell you that what happened to Meredith wasn't your fault. And I can tell you this, you may not need tennis, but tennis needs you."

"What do you mean?" Faith asked, confused.

"Everyone has a gift," Arthur explained. "Some people figure out what it is and use it to do great things. Some people never recognize their gifts. Tennis is *your* gift. You're a good tennis player, and you could be great. You can make a name for yourself and the sport. In return, tennis can give you a lot of things."

"Like pain?" Faith suggested. "That's what it gave Meredith."

"No," Arthur replied. "Her father did that. *He* broke her bones—and maybe her heart. But don't let him break you too. Don't let him break your spirit."

"I don't need tennis," Faith mumbled. "It's not that important."

Arthur smiled. "Tennis gave me a chance to change the world. It let me give hope to people who didn't have it. It helped me show the world that anyone could be a tennis champion, regardless of skin color. You'll help more people than you'll hurt by playing tennis, Faith. I promise. But it's a choice you'll have to make."

"I guess," Faith said, not sounding convinced. She wiped the tears from her cheeks and sniffed. "Are you gonna play?"

"Not tonight," Arthur said. "I just came here to talk."

"But you only have tonight and tomorrow!" Faith reminded.

"I know. But talking to you is more important."

"Oh," was all Faith could say.

"When I was alive, I had to have several operations," Arthur explained. "Then I got AIDS. Some days my body felt like it wanted to quit, but I wouldn't let it." Arthur paused and then added, "If you really want to play tennis, you won't let anything stop you."

Faith was quiet for a moment. She stared at a tennis ball lying on the court. She had a question for Arthur but wasn't quite sure how to put it.

"What's it like when you die?" she finally asked him cautiously.

"You see things a little clearer," Arthur quickly answered, as if expecting her question.

"What do you mean by 'clearer'?"

"You see what's really important," Arthur explained. "And you see how your decisions affected others. And you understand some of the good—and bad—things that happened in your life and how they changed you. Like I came to understand that the prejudice I faced made me a stronger person, one who was able to fight for the rights of others.

"What happened to your friend," Arthur continued, "is terrible, but if you let it stop you from playing tennis, you let the bad win. Someday I think you'll regret that."

"I never thought of it like that," Faith quietly remarked.

"Like I said," Arthur said, "you see things differently."

"You know, there's an old man who owns these courts," Faith began. "His name is Mr. West. He's a really nice guy. The other day he was telling me how much he used to love playing tennis. But now he can't play anymore because of his health. I was thinking that maybe hitting a few balls with him would make him feel better."

"Like I said," Arthur reminded, "sometimes you can change the world with a tennis racket. It really is true. Even if it's the world of just one person."

"Are you saying I should play with him?" Faith asked.

"That's up to you," Arthur said. He stood up and walked out to the court. He stopped at the back of the court, reached into his pocket, and pulled out a tennis ball. Bouncing it on the court, he continued, "I want to ask one last question. If you say no, I'll understand. But since tomorrow night's my last, I'd like to hit with you again. Do you think you could do that?"

"I guess," Faith agreed. She stood up and walked out to where Arthur was standing.

"I don't want you to feel bad about breaking your promise."

"I know," Faith said.

"I think a good promise is easy to keep," Arthur observed. He put the ball in his pocket. "The ones that are hard to keep . . . well, sometimes I just don't think they were meant to be promises."

"How do you know which ones are which?" Faith asked.

"You just do," Arthur said simply.

Faith was about to press for a better response when she heard footsteps behind her. Swinging around, she saw her dad walking down the path to the courts. Whipping back around, she found that Arthur had disappeared.

"Faith?" she heard her dad's familiar voice.

"Hi, Dad," Faith called out.

Mr. Long smiled and walked over to where she was standing. "The courts look beautiful, honey." He wrapped his arm around her shoulder and gave her a hug. "I'm proud of you, Faith. You do nice work."

"Thanks, Dad," Faith replied. "How'd you know I was here?"

"Just a guess. I was out for a walk and thought I might find you here. Mind if your old man walks you home?"

"Nope, let's go," Faith replied.

Together they walked off the court, past the barn, and down the hill. As they walked, Faith glanced around at the trees, the grass, the flowers, and the shadows. She was looking for a hint of Arthur—some clue to where he'd gone. But nothing seemed out of place. Faith hoped he'd be back tomorrow.

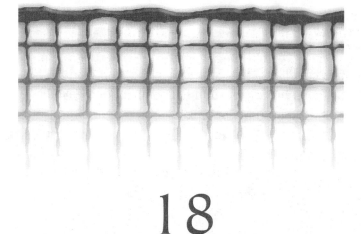

18

For most of the next day, Faith thought about what Arthur had told her. She remembered it while she swept the courts. It flashed through her mind at the library. She pondered it as she rode her bike home.

After supper, she told her dad she was going for a walk. She hurried to the club and stood looking around, waiting for Arthur to return. The sun had sunk below the tree line. The sky was a deep shade of violet.

After the first hour, Faith began to think Arthur wasn't coming. She decided to sweep the courts to kill some time. If no one played again tonight, she wouldn't have to come back in the morning.

When she was finished, Faith sat on the bench next to the court and watched the stars begin to pop out. When the sky turned black, she became more and more anxious. Impatiently, she continued to sit and wait in the moonlight.

"Arthur!" she called out softly. The night air whispered to her through the trees. Faith wondered if it was trying to tell her its secrets. She had trusted Arthur with all of her secrets, and he'd understood them. He seemed to understand *her*, which was more than any teacher or counselor had done.

"Arthur!" she yelled a little louder. Suddenly, the court lights flashed on. Light spilled onto the clay courts. Faith stood up, holding her racket, her head whipping from side to side. She spotted someone walking slowly up the hill. He had white hair and was wearing a white shirt and shorts. He was carrying a tennis racket. It was Mr. West.

"Evening, Faith," Mr. West greeted. "Beautiful night to play tennis."

"Uh-huh," Faith replied. She looked around, afraid Arthur might pop out and scare Mr. West.

"What's the matter? You look nervous. Something wrong?" Mr. West asked.

"No," Faith said. "Nothing. So who are you hitting with Mr. West?"

His eyebrows went up. He stopped walking and stared at Faith. He seemed a little confused by her question. "I got your note," Mr. West mumbled.

"My note?" Faith repeated.

"Yes, the one you left on the barn door," Mr. West explained. "It said you wanted to hit with me. Didn't you write it? Maybe it was one of the guys pulling my leg."

Faith felt terrible. She didn't know what to say. She watched the smile disappear from Mr. West's face. He shrugged his shoulders.

"It's okay. I'll just go inside and read a little," Mr. West sighed. He looked around at the courts and nodded. "They look good, Faith."

Faith felt awful as she watched Mr. West start to walk off the court. She felt torn. Should she break her promise again and hit with Mr. West? Was her promise a good one? Maybe . . .

"I'll hit with you." Faith couldn't believe the words that popped out of her mouth. But then a sense of peace filled her, and somehow she knew it was the right decision. The weight of the past few months lifted, and she felt like a new person.

Faith stood up and twirled her racket in her hand, something she hadn't done in months. She walked over to Mr. West and smiled.

"Are you sure?" he asked.

"I—I think so." Faith nodded. "Yes," she corrected, "I'm sure."

"What about your promise?"

"I've decided it wasn't good enough to keep," Faith answered.

Together they took to the court with smiles on

their faces and hit tennis balls for about an hour. Arthur never appeared—at least not in person. Faith had a feeling that he was there somewhere, watching and smiling.

When they finished, Faith felt better than she had all summer. And she could tell by the look on Mr. West's face that he felt good too. Faith knew Arthur had been right. She'd used tennis to make something good happen. She'd used her gift to make a difference in someone else's life. Now she understood.

19

A few days later, Mr. West was sitting on his chair in front of the barn. He was reading the newspaper when he spotted Faith walking up the hill.

Chapter Nineteen

"Hi, Faith!" Mr. West called out.

Faith just smiled and continued up the path to the front of the barn. "Morning, Mr. West," she said when she reached him.

"How's my tennis partner?" Mr. West smiled. "You ready to play again?"

"Actually, I came up to tell you I won't be able to sweep the courts next weekend."

"Really?" Mr. West asked. "Why?"

"My dad's driving me to a tennis tournament," Faith replied.

"A tournament?" Mr. West asked, a little surprised. "That sounds exciting. Are you watching or playing?"

"Playing," Faith said. "I may be kind of rusty, but I'm ready to get back into the swing of things. Hopefully, I'll be able to practice here a bit this week."

"So what changed your mind?" Mr. West asked.

"This place," Faith said, "and hitting with you. It was fun, and I realized how important tennis is to me."

"Me too," Mr. West agreed, grinning. "That was the best I've felt in years. Swinging a racket. Hitting the balls. Moving around the court again. I felt like a young man. I'm grateful to you."

"I think we're even then," Faith replied. She turned and looked up the path. "How are the courts?"

"The Nortons were here earlier," Mr. West said.

"I'll go check them," Faith said. She walked up to the courts and was surprised to see them swept and in perfect condition. Only one thing was out of place. A tennis ball lay on the court next to the net. She walked over and picked it up. COME TO THE FIELD, the ball read.

Faith turned and looked at the line of cornstalks next to the courts. She walked off the court and took a few steps into the cornfield. She looked around as she walked. After about ten steps, she found Arthur standing in the shadows of the cornstalks. When she got closer to him, she could see he was still dressed in the same white shirt and dark shorts. His arms were folded. He had a bright smile on his face.

"So how was it?" Arthur asked.

"It felt good," Faith admitted. "I knew it was the right thing to do."

"Yes, it was," Arthur agreed. "You remember the first time you asked me if I was a ghost? Remember what I said?"

"You said you were here to help me find something I lost," Faith recalled.

"That's right." Arthur nodded. "I think you've found it, Faith. I think you got your spark back."

"How can you be sure?" Faith asked.

"Let's check," Arthur suggested. He put his

116

hand in his short's pocket, like he always did for a tennis ball. This time, when he pulled his hand out, it was empty. Arthur looked down at his empty hand. Then he looked at Faith and smiled.

"Looks like I'm out of tennis balls," he said. "Guess it's time for me to go."

"Can't you stay?" Faith asked.

"I could try," Arthur replied, "but then I'd be breaking the rules. And if you've read anything about Arthur Ashe, then you know I always follow the rules. I have to go."

"Okay," Faith sighed. She felt sad knowing this was the last time she would see Arthur. A tear slid down her cheek.

"I'm gonna miss you," Arthur said. He glanced over Faith's shoulder at the courts. "I'll miss playing tennis out there too. This is such a beautiful place."

"What if something happens?" Faith asked. "What if I stop playing again? Will you come back? Will you help me again?"

Arthur held out his hand and a tennis ball appeared. He put the ball in Faith's hand. The word BELIEVE was printed on the ball in bright red letters.

"I want you to keep this," Arthur said. "Just to remind you I'll always listen. All you have to do is close your eyes and say my name, and you'll know I'm with you. Go ahead and try it. See if it works."

Faith felt a little silly. But she closed her eyes and said his name. No sooner had the name left her lips than she felt the ball grow warm. A tingle started in her hand and traveled up her arm. Her heart lifted and she smiled. When she opened her eyes, Arthur was gone.

Faith quickly closed her eyes again. The warm feeling returned. The tingle resumed in her arm. "Arthur," she whispered. She squeezed the ball tight. "Thank you."

"You're welcome," a windy voice replied.

Faith opened her eyes. The warm feeling was gone. She walked out of the field and onto the tennis courts. When she left these courts, Faith knew that she would take a part of them with her. Wherever she went to play tennis, Faith would always know it was because of two clay courts in Pennsylvania—and a friend named Arthur Ashe.

Dear Meredith,

I've decided to play tennis again. I will always feel terrible about what happened to you, but now I know it wasn't my fault. Tennis is a gift we both share. I hope we can play together again soon.

Faith

Library Media Center
Fegely Middle School